Praise for *In the Morni...*

"*In the Morning, the City Is the Prairie* is ... ...een through the eyes of college dropout M... ...real: spiked with skyscrapers and paved wi... ...ying earth beneath a boundless sky. Roensc... ...t me reading for the surprise of each sentence."

—**Chris Harding Thornton**, author of
Pickard County Atlas and *Little Underworld*

"Set during a recent, turbulent spring in Oklahoma City, Rob Roensch's engrossing new novel drops us into the rich, quirky mind of Matt, a college dropout/reluctant Costco cashier who's trying to figure out what and who is worth fighting for as his family—and the entire country, it seems—falls apart around him. Searching, funny, and wise, *In the Morning, the City Is the Prairie* is both a moving coming-of-age novel and an urgent investigation into what will actually be required if we're to remain hopeful in this beautiful, broken world."

—**Mark Rader**, author of
The Wanting Life

Praise for *The World and the Zoo*

"Rob Roensch is the Jim Jarmusch of Central Oklahoma zoo-fiction—contemplative and dreamy and in awe of the strange. . . . This book's tenderness amplifies the tenderness of being on the outer edge of being young—where nights are wide open and everything seems to be beginning and ending and straining toward the future."

—**Benjamin Warner**, author of
Thirst and *Fearless*

"Roensch's writing style is captivating and fresh, with deft description that is both terse and enchanting. This is first-rate writing."

—**Bobbie Ann Mason**, author of
The Girl in the Blue Beret and *Dear Ann*

"When the accumulation of facts and experience fails to locate truths and purpose, a sense of the ineffable is always available, a sense of wonder."

—**Joe Sacksteder**, *DIAGRAM*

in the morning, the city is the prairie

in the morning,
the city is the prairie

rob roensch

a novel

Fort Smith, Arkansas

IN THE MORNING, THE CITY IS THE PRAIRIE

Cover art by Chad Reynolds

Edited by Casie Dodd
Design & typography by Belle Point Press

Belle Point Press, LLC
Fort Smith, Arkansas
bellepointpress.com
editor@bellepointpress.com

Find Belle Point Press
on Facebook,
Twitter (@BellePointPress),
and Instagram (@bellepointpress)

Printed in the United States of America

27 26 25 24 23   1 2 3 4 5

Library of Congress Control Number: 2023947932

ISBN: 978-1-960215-09-3

IMCP/BPP19

For Carrie and Tully and Penny

oklahoma city, 2018

Monday

I T'S THE LAST cool night of spring. Connor declares he is going to become
a poet by fall. He has hooked his knees around the top bar of the swing
set and is hanging upside down. He's still wearing his suit; his tie dangles
and shimmers. I haven't taken off my Costco name tag.

"You can't just decide to be someone," I say. I'm on a swing drifting back
and forth at the speed of a cradle.

"We're 23," he says. "This is America. *You* say something you're going to
be by September."

"I don't know," I say. "The same. Alive."

WHEN I get home all the lights in the house are on. The storm door is
slightly open, a limp sail. I can hear my parents arguing before I open the
door. I'm high enough that I want to see what's going on more than I'm
worried that I'm too high. I go in and my younger sister Sylvie, a few weeks
away from graduating high school, is alone in the living room in pajama
pants and the Thunder T-shirt from the year they lost in the finals that
she wears all the time even though she hates basketball. It's not that she's
never awake this late, but that she's never both awake and visible. Next to
her on the big beige TV couch are two large boxes and one that is wider
and flatter. She doesn't look up from her phone.

My parents' arguing voices echo in from the bright never-bright hall to
the bedrooms. "What's going on?" I say to my sister.

"See for yourself," she says. Something teenager important is happening
inside the phone. Her thumbs twitch fevered and graceful.

"What's in the boxes?" I say.

"Treasure," she says.

"You could just tell me," I say.

"I could," she says. She doesn't.

Down the hall, my mother's voice says: "So put it on the other card." They are in my room. I make my way into the hall. "We'll figure it out," she says. "We always do."

"What other card do you think we have?" says my father.

"We'll get another!"

"Claire," says my father in the voice he only uses for her name.

"Don't 'Claire' me," says my mother. The large framed print of a horse against the sunset that has been on the wall next to my bedroom door all my life is on the floor leaning in the bathroom doorway. I have never been on a horse. The glass is cracked across its face in two neat wavy lines. The empty space on the wall glows.

I peek into my room.

My father and mother don't notice me. Their antlers are stuck together. There is sweat on their faces. The frame and mattress of my bed are on their sides on the wrong side of the room, where the desk I didn't use was but now is not. Where my bed was there is another bed, narrower and taller, with gray plastic rails. Some kind of adjustable hospital bed. It is too large for the room, like a tennis ball in a mouth, and tall enough to block half the window that looks out onto the back yard and the dogwood and the shed and its hidden opossum. In the new bed—half sitting up, leaning back, underneath stiff, turned-down white sheets—is my Aunt Becky, my father's sister, whom I have not seen since I was a child but remember right away because she is my father with a sharper face. Because of her, the year I was seven the phone rang so often in the middle of the night that when I woke up in the dark and the house was quiet I was afraid. She once sent my sister a birthday card from a prison in Texas my father would not let her read. Aunt Becky smiles at me.

"Matt. You're high," she says.

"Hi," I say, hearing the repetition. "Hello," I say. My father turns to me; my mother doesn't.

"You're gonna have to crash in the living room," he says. "It shouldn't be for long."

"David!" says my mother.

"I'll be out of your hair before you know it," says Aunt Becky.

"It's my room," I say, out of what even I can hear is baked wonder. There is a new fizzy white smell.

"It's his room," says my father to my mother, defending me as he never does.

"You're the one who wanted to throw him out!" says my mother.

"What?" I say.

"I'm dying," says Aunt Becky.

"Me too," I say. My mother looks at me. "I don't know why I said that," I say. Aunt Becky grins. One of her upper front teeth is missing.

"You *are* high," she says.

Tuesday

IN THE MORNING I wake up and realize I heard my mother's voice.

"What?" I say.

"Don't you have work?" she says. I can tell it's ten because of the quality of light in my closed eyes.

"Don't *you*?" I say.

"I took the day," she says. She never takes the day.

"Not until noon," I say.

"Why are you on the floor?" she says. I remember that last night, for some reason, it would have been beneath my dignity to sleep on the couch.

"It's better," I say. I open my eyes and Simon, our seal-sleek, pillow-sized black mutt, is delighted. His tail thwaps the leg of the coffee table he has been underneath, and he scoots his head forward to lick my face.

I feel I've been observed, like a psychiatric patient. I wonder if I've been talking in my sleep and what I said.

"Did you walk Simon?" I say.

"Ask him," she says. She's wearing her cheerful-yard-work sweatpants and sweatshirt, but she's not cheerful.

"Is Aunt Becky still here?" I say.

"What kind of a question is that?" she says.

"Why couldn't you give her Sylvie's room? She's younger."

"You know Sylvie needs her space. All you do in your room is sleep."

"That's not true. I read. I practice guitar."

"Sylvie's had your guitar in her room since winter and you haven't seemed to care. And there's been a World Religions textbook on your floor open to the same page for months."

"I was gonna read that."

"'The Meaning of Suffering.' You circled it."

"It was like that when I got it. And why are you reading my book?"

"Someone should. Listen, we're all going to have to make sacrifices."

"Dad didn't want her here at all, did he?"

"It's cancer. It's partly cancer. She's lived a hard life. You know that, right?"

"I'm not seven."

"She doesn't have long."

"So it was your idea she's here."

"It's what Becky wants," she says. "I'm just the person who said it out loud."

"Why you?"

"It's the right thing to do," she says. She once made me apologize to a CVS cashier for snatching a lollipop I thought was free. I was three.

"Is Dad at work?" I say.

"If she asks you to help her die, say no, okay?"

"Jesus."

"Promise me, Matthew Bennet."

"Fine. Where's Dad?"

"He's out in his fucking kayak," she says.

"You don't swear," I say.

"Walk the dog," she says.

SIMON loves to pull on his leash but he's so old it's hard for him to get far enough ahead of me, so I have to walk very slowly. Everyone else on the street with a dog lets it out in the back yard, but Simon insists on the front door, the world. Without him, I would not truly live in my neighborhood. We mostly walk in the street because there's no sidewalk. The two houses that have had *For Sale* signs for six months still have *For Sale* signs; the vacant rental on the corner has weeds as tall as children. Everything here is stuck and aging: the leaves of the pecan trees shiver; the basketball hoop over the Gardners' garage wilts.

Aunt Becky doesn't fit here; she's dying, but she's new.

I admire how eagerly Simon presses the moist, gray-bristled face of his nose directly into specific bare patches of neighbors' front yards, as if he could breathe earth. Some part of him is still young. "You could become a great poet by fall," I tell him.

WHEN I get back to the house, my mother is in the kitchen angrily contemplating a pot of water on to boil. Only very occasionally does the labor behind her patience become so visible. My hair reflected in the mirror by the door looks like stapled squirrels. I unclick the dog and he totters to the center of the room and collapses, content.

"You should get some rest," I say to my mother.

"Who else is going to look after your Aunt Becky today?" she says. "You?"

"I'm on at noon," I say.

"We all do the best we can," she says. I don't say that's obviously not true.

AFTER a shower that's only intermittently warm despite the knob turned all the way up to H, as has recently become typical, I'm on my way to work when the house says my name.

The door to my room is cracked open, and I nudge it open more and stand in the doorway. The old bed and the new bed are where they were. My clothes have been piled by the closet door. It's like the room was never my room. I never put anything back on the walls when I moved back in after dropping out of college.

Aunt Becky is in her bed. She looks the same.

"Don't try to steal my pain pills," she says.

"I won't," I say.

"You're 23, right?" she says.

"I guess so," I say.

"You don't know?"

"I gotta get to work."

"Your father doesn't keep liquor or beer in the house, does he?"

8

"My mom doesn't like him when he drinks beer. They drink wine with dinner sometimes."

"Most days, I like a little beer. It's been months."

"Did you ask my mom?"

"Are you 23 or 12?"

"I don't know if I should."

"And nothing fancy," she says. "I'm not the queen."

"Could have fooled me," I say. I expect her to snap back, but she doesn't.

"Come talk to me, sometime," she says. "Okay? I get bored."

"Okay," I say.

I CAN get full-time hours at Costco some weeks since the band broke up and I don't put in requests for evenings off anymore. I miss the band, but not having it makes the days simpler. What I make pays for my car (a Scion, a lumpy black cube they don't even make anymore with 100,000 miles on it) and some rent for my parents. I'm still on my parents' health care. I have no plans other than keeping my job. I have completed 2.3 years of college with a 2.3 GPA. My last semester, I failed my Gen Ed Ethics course for not writing an essay I had plenty of time to write. I used to be able to write pages and pages of appropriate bullshit for any assignment. One afternoon I sat at a window in the library and stared at a blank page for an hour. Then I wrote the words, "This doesn't matter." Across the quad, the windows of the business school gleamed like hell in the sunset. I wanted like I was dying of thirst to get high and listen to music, so I did not die of thirst.

When I get out of my car in the Costco parking lot, there is a text from Connor: a photo of a row of endless stair machines at his gym; beyond the machines is a mirror the size of a lake.

At work, I text back.

Still awake, he responds.

Inside, Boss Jessica is whacking a glitching walkie talkie on a corner of Register 4. She knows everything about error codes and return policies and inventory. She is wearing the Darth-Vader-Kitten-Face T-shirt. His green eyes watch me from between the halves of the red Costco vest. I admire always his cruel kitten efficiency. I know she has a Fleetwood Mac CD stuck in the stereo of her Ford Focus and it still works. The guest checking out is a thin blue-jeaned man with a flat full of boxed whole milk and one 6-pack of packing tape. Behind him the line stretches to bulk candy.

"You want me to count in and open 5?" I say on my way by.

"Honey, you read my mind," she says.

I AM as fast now at counting out the till as anyone. The trick is giving in to the machine in yourself.

I get a good size line before I even flick on. America is always in line and watching for another open lane, another cashier, and I am that cashier. The belt is always full; I have numbers in the tips of my fingers. I would describe work hours, when it's busy, as not unpleasant. I don't have to think.

I decide without trying to that Aunt Becky would prefer Coors Light—the Silver Bullet.

At some point three boxes of rolls of Wintergreen lifesavers appear on the belt. They were always around my house, but I never learned they sparked in the dark until I went away to college. Then three sets of white bedsheets, an electric blanket. I look up, and it's my father. He smells like a pond. Sunglasses hang from a cord around his neck. I know there are wet items in the extra pockets of his cargo shorts, an 18-pack of paper towels under the cart.

"I was wondering when you'd notice," he says.

"I was focused," I say, scanning.

"Always could be when you decided to be," he says. My father almost understands me. He often says things like, "The only reason you go to work on time is so I won't throw you out for coming home high the night before," which is not completely wrong, but he doesn't know what it feels like to lie on the floor in the dark with enough music in the headphones to erase the rest of the world. He is not exactly an accountant, but the word "payroll" is involved in his job. He was out of work for a year and a half when I was in high school. When I was a child, he read me many books about space exploration.

"It's $77.82," I say. He digs out a credit card from a deep pocket of his wallet, jams it in, frowning. "Is this stuff for Aunt Becky?"

He fixes me so hard in his eyes I can almost feel his hands on my shoulders. "You should know," he says. "What she did. Some things can't be forgiven."

"What exactly did she do?" I say.

"Did you get the paper towels?" he says.

"I got the paper towels."

"The ones under the cart?"

"I always get the paper towels," I say.

"Your mother's got a good heart, Matt. All that church stuff. She actually believes it." I almost say, *why do you go with her then if that's the way you feel about it?* But I don't. I understand—he goes because he goes.

"You want the receipt?" He takes it.

"Keep your eyes open around your aunt, okay?"

"She's stuck in bed," I say.

"You think it makes me happy, having to say things like this?" he says, moving along like any customer, on his way.

I'm out on carts before my first break and there, emerging around the corner of a mobile-home-sized SUV, is Jane. I'm always surprised by how happy it makes me to see her. She is pretty and direct as daylight. She is what I miss most about the band breaking up—not the spark of seeing Dream Nerve in the *Gazette* gig listings—or even the music itself, those few moments when I felt like I was creating a song, not fighting my fingers—but Jane, near the front, to the side, precisely two-beer flushed, bright in the dark. She is extremely well organized and professional during the day, but has an appreciation for loud music, in certain hours, that I am grateful for, or else we never would have met. She's wearing sunglasses on her head and the same candy-red WE ARE OKLAHOMA T-shirt she's been wearing for the past week. She's in her first year of teaching fifth grade and recently walked out with the rest of the teachers in protest of their terrible pay, and in protest of the condition of education funding in the state in general. It's not terribly surprising how little Oklahoma pays teachers; what is surprising is that anyone is trying to do anything about it. Today is her second day of participating in the state-wide walkout, and in the protest at the Capitol. They won't succeed. It's Oklahoma. It's America.

"You have any boxes for me?" Jane says, all business. "We need boxes."

"Good to see you, too," I say.

"Can you go grab some?"

"I'm prohibited from abandoning my responsibilities," I say.

"I'm a customer who needs help," she says.

"Yes, ma'am," I say. We're already heading in; the snake of carts can rest in its corral for five minutes.

"I've gotta buy some granola bars and more markers, too," she says.

"Don't spend any money on markers," I say. "I have a present for you."

While she pays for the granola bars, I load a flat with uncrushed boxes from the pile waiting for the compactor and snag the opened-and-marked-as-a-loss and still perfectly good pack of 23-of-24 multi-colored Sharpies I have in my locker. I often rescue art supplies for her. I have carefully retaped the package closed so it looks new.

It seems like all the boxes won't fit in her little white car, but then I shift things around and sing a little song about the boxes, and they do fit.

When I'm done, she's examining where I've sealed the pack of multi-colored Sharpies. She's got her sunglasses flicked down over her eyes. There's something else she has to say.

"What?" I say.

"I don't know if I can do this," she says.

"You don't know if you can do what?" I say.

"This."

"Putting boxes in your car?"

"We never see each other. And it's going to be like this forever."

"It's a good job."

"What do you even do this for?"

"You know. You go to work to pay for things," I say. "I got you that atlas."

"The atlas. Right. You think it's going to be like this forever, don't you? Me visiting you in this parking lot? And that's okay?" I'm smart enough in the moment not to argue.

"I could get a different job," I say.

"It's not about the job. The only friend you talk to is that weird guy Connor. You don't even play music anymore."

"I wasn't any good," I say. "And I like Connor."

"I do, too. That's not the point."

"I'm off early tomorrow," I say. "I'll come see you down there after. Okay?"

"At the protest this morning, there were these motorcycle guys with Confederate flags revving their engines."

"Were they lost Civil War re-enactors?"

"This isn't a joke!" she says.

"I'm sorry," I say. "I know it's important to you. I think you deserve a raise. I do."

"It's not about the money!"

"I just don't think anything's going to change."

"How can you believe that?" she says.

"Alright. I'll call in sick tomorrow. I'll go," I say. "For you."

"I don't want you to do anything you don't want to do," she says.

"I want to," I say.

"Do you?" she says.

I MET Jane for the first time after a house show off 10th Street last April. She was with a nervous volleyball-player blonde compulsively biting the side of her lip; Jane, in authoritatively carnation-pink jeans, was not nervous, but so distinct from the rest of the ragged crush that she was spotlit. She told me she thought she recognized me. In retrospect, I don't think she was attempting to flirt—Jane will simply say what is in her mind—but I convinced myself, luckily, because otherwise I would have realized too soon that she was out of my league. I was sweaty from playing our four best songs;

we hadn't played well, but we'd played as loud as we could. I was about to come on way too strong to her, but before I could say something stupid there were two cops at the door and there was a general scramble and Jane was all at once as nervous as her friend (it turned out they were both in their semester of student teaching and had of course never been in any sort of trouble). Because I was not afraid, I perhaps appeared brave. The best I can say for myself is that I am not *not* brave. I shepherded her and her friend through the torn-out kitchen to the back door and promised to make sure they had time to get away safe while I made my way back to the front door to stand with a shirtless kid with silver eyebrows to briefly argue with the cops and then begrudgingly agree to disperse.

At our next show opening for the openers at Lost Train Collective, Jane was there, and alone, and we were off.

We would never have met otherwise. Her parents used to be in the Air Force.

The summer that followed was the best of my life. In the evenings Jane sought out loud music, and getting a little drunk, and me, with deliberate purpose. And I loved music, and lights in the dark, and Jane, and getting almost but not quite too drunk.

That August she started having to get up early. Then the band broke up, and I traded the bass for a used alternator and some medium-good weed, and I took on more hours at Costco.

I visited her classroom a few days before school started. I have never seen such perfect construction-paper cut-out letters. Over the windows: "WHERE IS YOUR ATTENTION?"

AFTER work, the first it-shouldn't-be-this-warm-already night—steamy haze of gnats under the parking lot streetlights—I call Jane and she doesn't pick up. I know she's asleep already and her phone is in its place, silent, charging at a right angle to her laptop on her little kitchen table.

I text Connor.

I'm everywhere, he says. I ask him if he wants to smoke up but there's no response.

WHEN I get home, my mother and father are sitting together on the couch. I have several warm Silver Bullets for my aunt in my pockets. The empty packaging from the sheets is piled on the seat of the recliner, an empty wine glass on the carpet next to my mother's foot. She is leaning on my father's shoulder, and they are watching the local news. My father's other hand is resting on top of the remote, which is resting on the cushion next to him. I recognize the aftermath of an argument; more often than not, their fights end when they get tired of arguing and watch something on TV that one or both of them are clearly not interested in.

One of the news anchors has golden-retriever hair. She throws to an interview with a shiny-haired oil company PR type who is less angry than disappointed, as in a child who should know better, by the recent proposal to fund teacher raises through a return of gross production tax levels to pre-fracking-boom levels. There are long shots of the state Capitol grounds mobbed with teachers in the red T-shirts. One of them, I know, is Jane. I of course can't pick her out. It's as if not finding her means I'm failing her. My father mutters, "No one put a gun to their head and forced them to take that job."

"Hush," says my mother.

Then, a closer shot: a choir-sized crowd of protesting teachers, mostly women in the red T-shirts. At first I think they're singing, but the song continues when the news cuts to the sports guy with the wide-open eyes. The song is my sister playing what used to be my guitar, and she's not in her room with the door closed. She is singing for Aunt Becky.

Simon wobbles toward me, his tail the hand of a clock, his face a tired question. He is always just about to know how to speak. "Hold on, dude," I say.

I stash the beer for Aunt Becky in the back of the fridge behind a half-empty two-liter of ginger ale and follow the sound of my guitar. I can't help but notice it's tuned correctly; it likes Sylvie more than me.

The hallway to my room is dark, but there is light from my room that is not my room anymore. I stand in the doorway and see that Aunt Becky is very asleep. I am obscurely disappointed. Next to her bed is a new alien hat rack—I guess for IV bags—but there is nothing hanging from it. Her head is tilted to the side, and her mouth is not wide open but fallen open, slack. There are some bruises around one wrist, and her skin there is loose and crumpled like wet newspaper dried out. Her hands rest on top of the new electric blanket that has been spread over her. It's not, for the moment, plugged in.

Sylvie is sitting on the black swivel chair that belonged to the desk that has been removed from the room and is looking into the carpet, dis-associating herself from herself in concentration. I am impressed or annoyed by her songs—what I can't help but hear of them through her closed door—depending on the atmosphere in my brain. She is an enthusiastic though not entirely accurate strummer, and she sings on key except for the notes she can't reach that she insists on trying to reach. She is attempting to form a band with her friends called Zoos of Fluorescent Anarchy. It's her and two other girls who don't sing as well as she does, one who has a saxophone. They have never played anywhere except in her room with the door closed or at her friend's house when no one else was home. They were supposed to play in someone's back yard one night, but she came home early with a tear-streaked face and didn't want to talk about it; I know she chickened out. They even made T-shirts to sell and didn't sell any, so I bought two; the T-shirt is green and has an octopus on it.

"The forests are all melting," she sings. "The water's dying clear. We will wait for you forever. We will wait for you right here."

Soon enough she hears me listening and looks up, locks her mouth closed, keeps strumming, but only as loud as bees. I see that there is a new streak of bright blue in her hair.

"I like that one," I say.

"Leave us alone," she says, whispering.

"I'm serious," I say, more quietly. "What's wrong with me telling you a song is good?"

"You don't actually care what it's saying."

"Sure I do."

"What were the Standing Rock protests about?"

"Native American water!"

"What does that mean?"

"I don't know, but, I mean, water is good, right?"

"See?" she says. "You don't care."

"You know she's asleep," I say.

"She woke up last time I stopped."

"I wasn't making fun of you," I say.

"Fine," she says. "Thank you." And she mouths, silently, "Go away."

WHEN I go back to the living room, my parents are gone, and the TV is off. I am often alone at this hour of the night. I am not often alone and listening to my sister singing songs maybe about the end of the world to my dying aunt in the room I slept in when I was a child. I feel a rumble of thunder against the skin of my throat. Simon presses his nose to my ankle, a gesture that signals his fear of storms. "I'll protect you," I tell him.

On the way back from our walk under a rumpled and flashing sky, I see that Connor's sleek black dart of a car is parked diagonally in our driveway, headlights off and purple spaceship undercarriage lights glowing like something I drew when I was nine. I unclick Simon inside the house to burrow under the coffee table. My sister is singing loud enough for me to hear but not loud enough for me to understand. I close the door and head back to Connor's car.

"It's gonna storm," I say as I get in.

"We're going to the top of the Devon Tower," he says.

"Whatever," I say.

CONNOR got his degree in finance a year early, the year I dropped out, and now works sometimes at First Oklahoma and sometimes for himself doing things I don't understand. He knows I am uncomfortable around cocaine. We were freshman-year-assigned roommates and are still friends because I always say *okay* and because, though he wouldn't admit it, he gets lonely.

Once, before we were really friends, I watched him make so many comments to the kid next to him during a Psych 100 lecture that the kid got up and switched seats—but Connor didn't notice, so when he turned again with a few words to share the kid was gone. I saw Connor's face. We ate together many terrible breakfasts. He is not unkind.

In the car he knows every word of every hip-hop song. Instead of saying the n-word he opens his mouth for the correct amount of time. His headlight-brights are like holding onto a flashlight that is the sun.

The Tower is the tallest building in Oklahoma City. From the outside, the glass gleams the blue-green of what people used to think the future would be. We park in the attached garage in one of the restricted spots he seems to think belongs to him. A few steps and we are in the lobby, a vast space in a hollowed-out honeycomb spaceship, deserted at that hour; I think for some reason of the interior rooms of the pyramids, vast and intricate tombs. He's wearing a black suit, though without a tie, and I'm still in my work khakis, though I changed into a T-shirt with baked-in paint splatter from my first post-college job painting houses. He shows his card to the security guard, and we are in the elevator. The elevator glides on a river up. He's talking fast about how tall buildings are built, how in order to build a skyscraper it's necessary to invent a way to reach above where the building is being built to be able to lower beams into place; to build something tall, you have to conceive of something taller; it's a metaphor for America; it's a metaphor for capitalism; it's a metaphor for how to live.

"Is this part of a poem?" I say.

"It's all part of it," he says. "It's all one poem."

"This elevator is cool," I say. Connor licks the wall.

"I thought so," he says.

The doors sweep open to a darkened and marble-floored lobby—the restaurant at the top of the tower, where I have never been. We are so high up shadows could be bottomless holes. The storm light flashes from windows I can't see.

"Power out?" I say.

"The restaurant's closed for a remodel," he says. "But I know the guy."

"Are we even allowed to be up here?"

"You have to stop living like there's someone out there in charge of what you can and can't do."

"Isn't there?"

"I told you. I know the guy."

"Isn't it dangerous in a storm?"

"You think the people who designed this tower didn't understand wind?"

Connor wanders across the lobby into the darkness of the darkly tiled restaurant like he knows where everything is. I navigate my way in the flashes behind him, barking a knee on a chair, until there is enough difference in shadow and space from the ambient light of the city seeping up for me to see. He makes his way to the wall of window, and I meet him there.

Then I can see the universe. The storm is passing to our north and not above us, but at our eye level. Within the darkness, there is another distinct darkness lit intermittently by lightning. The perspective allows me to see how defined and limited the storm is; it is only clouds, not the sky. The lines of light of the city below us stretch in a grid in every direction, weak yellow, like squished fireflies streaked on asphalt with a finger. Everything is small except for the night. Somewhere out in the night is my dying aunt, and Jane.

I turn and Connor is gone. I hear in the vague distance furniture shifting, a clinking. He comes back presently with two opened beers and hands one to me.

"No king ever had a view like this," he says.

"Unless he got on a plane," I say.

"You should come work for me," he says. "Make big money."

It's not the first time he's offered. It's impossible. "I'm doing okay," I say.

"I could teach you," he says. "I know how everything works."

"Sometimes I get to run the cardboard compactor," I say.

"You can't be a dropout forever."

"Why not?" I say. "What, like, I should be sitting at a computer all day watching numbers fly around?"

"That's money," says Connor. "That's what money is. That's what built this tower to stand in the storm. That's what got us up here."

Lightning flashes below us.

Wednesday

I N T H E M O R N I N G I wake up to find I am still resolved to visit Jane at the teacher protest at the Capitol and to stay the day with her. Before I give myself time to generate an excuse or let the feeling pass, I call in to say I'm sick, which feels strange because I've never done it before. I never want to go to work, but it's easier just to go.

The house is less empty but more quiet than usual at that hour: my father is at work, my sister is at school (I imagine scrawling song lyrics in ballpoint pen on the undersides of her wrists), and Simon is asleep on the recliner—someone else has already walked him. On my way to brush my teeth and shower, I see that someone—my mother—has dumped the clothes from the pile that was in front of my closet into a pile in the hall. This is lucky because otherwise I wouldn't have changed clothes. I have a flash of worry that I'm the only one in the house to look after my aunt, but in the next instant I know my mother must have taken more time off from her new job answering phones at the Love's corporate office; she must be somewhere in the house—maybe napping in her room—because no one ever depends on me for anything.

I recognize even as I am thinking it that there is no reason for me to feel as I do that it is very important that I leave the house as quickly as possible.

As I'm about to open the front door out I hear, like a memory, the tinkling of a bell, as from a bicycle in an old movie—a sound that is both small and ghostly, a corner-of-the-eye sound, not real. But I know I did hear it. I wait and hear it again. A bell. My mother does not appear.

I could leave, but I follow the sound.

My bedroom door is closed; I start to crack it open and then I think, *what am I doing?* This is my room. So I swing the door open. I don't know what I'm expecting to find—myself, sprawled out on top of the sheets, asleep. But I'm nowhere. Aunt Becky is there, of course, halfway propped up in the new bed. At the foot of the bed now is a table I don't recognize, on top of which is the TV from my parents' room. A chaotic puddle of wires on the carpet. There's also a little table next to her bed now, another one I don't recognize, on top of which is the remote for the TV, the giant plastic tumbler with a top and attached straw my mother drinks iced tea out of, and the bell—brass colored, with a black stick for a handle. I have also never seen the bell before. The world is leaking into my house.

"Hi, Aunt Becky," I say.

"Your mother must be asleep," she says.

"I don't know," I say.

"She'd be in here already if she was awake," says Aunt Becky, "putting the back of her hand on my forehead to check for fever like this was Little House on the Damn Prairie." She pauses. "She still does that for you, doesn't she?"

I'm again impressed by the speed and accuracy of her character diagnosis. "She likes to help," I say.

"You got me some beer?"

"Yeah. It's in the fridge."

"Well?" she says. It takes me a second.

"You want it now? At ten in the morning?"

"What do I care what time of day it is?"

"Hold on."

"I'll wait here."

When I get back with the cold Coors Light, she's holding down the button that is lifting her all the way to sitting. I pop the beer for her and pass it over. She takes it carefully in two hands because it is very heavy. "Good boy," she says. At first I think she's going to drain the whole thing, but she takes one slurping sip and grimaces, then one shoulder starts to tremble and I have to reach forward to take the can before she drops it. I set it on the table. She closes her eyes and leans back into the pillow.

"Something wrong?" I say. She runs her tongue along the inside of her upper lip and opens her eyes and regards me.

"What has your father told you about me?" she says.

"Nothing," I say, lying.

"You're lying," she says.

"Not much."

"Do you want to hear a story about your father?"

"I have to go to work," I say, and she smiles a strange smile, like a little kid about to tell a joke, and she's about to start telling me the story, but then it's like her smile hurts, and she closes her eyes. "Are you okay?" I say.

"Can you get me some ice water?"

I return the beer to the back of the fridge and fill up her water tumbler.

When I come back to the room, she's reclined the bed again and her eyes are still closed, but she's not asleep.

"Can I get you anything else?" I say.

"I need to rest," she says. The skin of her face is very dry, and her mouth is very wet. I have the urge to rest the back of my own hand against her forehead, the way my mother would.

"Okay," I say and, because I don't know what else to say, "Good night."

In the hallway on my way out my mother appears, hair wild with a quick sleep. She glares at me like I've done something wrong and of course I have, though she has no way of actually knowing, and she darts past me into Aunt Becky's room.

"I have to go to work," I tell her. There is no response.

In the car I realize I have no idea how to get to the state Capitol building even though I have seen it from the highway a million times, so I have to look up the map of the city I live in on the phone. Like my father, for no reason I refuse to use the app that tells you where to drive as you drive.

I drive through traffic I drive through all the time, past the bad Sonic and the good Sonic, and then I don't get on the highway but take less familiar city streets and all of a sudden I'm sweeping toward the back of the Capitol. It's more unreal in real life: ridiculously serious, Roman off-white, a grand dome topped by a statue the size of a person who is not afraid to be up so high. It looks like a movie set. When I'm still some distance away, the side streets become packed full of parked cars, school buses, charter buses, church vans. I get closer and see the crowds of people all over the grounds on all sides of the Capitol itself. It's like there's a music festival except, I realize, the crowd is not as mostly-white, which probably says something about the music festivals I've been to. There are tailgate tents here and there. Kids holding posterboard signs out for passing traffic to read: "Save Our Futures!" "Oklahoma is NOT OK!" "HONK IF YOU HAD A PUBLIC SCHOOL TEACHER WHO CHANGED YOUR LIFE." I honk and remember Coach T, a square man who taught PE and got fired for slapping a sophomore girl on the butt. But that isn't fair—there's also Mrs. Peabody, who almost got me to enjoy Shakespeare by reading the most violent parts out loud and doing voices, even on days we were supposed to be doing test prep—and Mr. Mahoney, who teared up when he talked about the letters home from soldiers who died in the Civil War. They were people who tried, like Jane. But what they taught didn't connect to my life, to my parents arguing in the kitchen after midnight, to traffic in the city. And it didn't connect to what I loved: what is a photocopy of a textbook page against the feeling of walking into a dark house full of noise with electricity in your blood?

Or maybe there's something wrong with me.

Through the window, I hear the dim buzz of someone talking through a loudspeaker, so I roll down the window, but I'm too far away to make out words. On the sidewalk, walking toward the crowd, there's a man in a windbreaker carrying six pizzas, a man pushing a woman in a wheelchair, a line of fifteen or so maybe-second graders wearing the red T-shirt, holding hands to stay connected. I can't think of any other time I've seen so many people wearing the same shirt. It's more strange to me than inspiring, though I do know I should be inspired. Two silver-sunglasses bicycle cops drift up the sidewalk, against foot traffic, parting the flow.

I have to continue several blocks south, past the unnecessary and so accurately symbolic, only-one-in-the-nation-on-Capitol-grounds functional oil pump nodding like a sleepy zombie, past packed parking lots until the parked cars lining the side streets start to thin out. I park on a side street in front of what even I can tell is an elegantly proportioned brick house but with boarded-up windows and a yard crawling with ivy and climbing weeds, set off from the sidewalk by a black iron fence with botanical spikes. None of the buildings in Oklahoma City are old; even its ruins are obviously temporary—either the neighborhood will ride a wave of oil-boom investment and be reinvented, or the wind and weeds will overcome everything. The unpredictable, enormous sky and the gently troubled flatness of the land are the only true permanents.

The weather is too warm; it's fair to assume the possibility of afternoon storms. The sky is scattered with torn-off hunks of cottony clouds, a familiar false peace. I make my way to the sidewalk on Lincoln and head north. I realize after a few blocks I'm the only one walking alone. Up ahead, the speaker has finished, and the loudspeaker is now offering a tinny "We Are Family" by Sister Sledge. It's exactly what it would sound like to be standing outside a church multi-purpose room wedding reception after celebrating the marriage of an unpleasant cousin. I walk past a group of middle-aged women—elementary school teachers probably—assembled on a rise on the grassy bank separating a parking lot from the street—and they are actually dancing. One has a bottle of blue Gatorade in one of the hands she is holding up to the side of her head as she rocks back and forth on her hips; another is singing out loud as if the words mean something.

I'm at the edge of the main crowd, still way more than rock-throwing distance away from the Capitol, before I understand that my plan to simply spot Jane will not be the work of a moment. Texting her will be useless. *Bet you aren't checking your phone*, I try, and stare at the words for a minute. No answering little dots. I step off the sidewalk up a grassy rise next to a twisted, solemn, adolescent pokey-needled pine to observe the crowd as a whole. There is a courtyard space in front of the Capitol, wide and deep, more or less full of people, most of them wearing the red T-shirts. The mass of people extends along the grounds around both wings of the building—covering the grass, surrounding the statues. I know there are more people present than I would guess; we imagine a person takes up more space than she does. In reality, humans are the size of a chair, half a deer, a couple boxes of diapers, a Christmas tree.

The wide steps up to the great doors are blocked off by bulky plastic Jersey barriers—not against demonstration, but because they have been closed for repairs for as long as even I, someone who doesn't pay attention to such things, can remember.

As I watch, I see that the crowd is moving through itself in a great loop along the sidewalk that circles the Capitol; the people marching are of the crowd and through the crowd. It's mesmerizing, biological, less a parade than a waterfall pouring into a lake. I can't think of another time I've encountered a crowd with a purpose that was not simply to stand and watch. It's a little frightening.

Before I see Jane, I spot at the far edge of the crowd a young woman speaking animatedly, incandescent with anger, her fingers tearing off pieces of the air as she walks. It's Jane. She has her hair neatly pulled back like she's at work. She's talking to a bearded young stork-man who is stupidly wearing his red teacher T-shirt over a long-sleeve collared shirt. Even from the distance I can see his face is bathed in sweat. He's listening to Jane too enthusiastically. I'm jealous first but then, and more deeply, confused. Why don't I know who she's talking to? Why don't I have any idea what she's saying?

I descend into the crowd and find myself swimming upstream. A bull-horn blarps on. It's a high school kid: "I'm not here for myself!" she says. "I'm here for my sisters!" She's in a mode of righteous whine, not unlike my own sister getting mad at me for using a plastic bag and not the reusable beeswax cloth she got for all of us for Christmas to rewrap the grocery store block of cheddar I only wanted a couple gnaws at. I know I'm being ungenerous. I salmon finally through the stagnant part of the mob into the march along the sidewalk. I spot the back of the bearded Jane-listener first. One flap of his button-down shirt is flapping out behind him, which pleases me, as if I am not myself a deep doofus.

I haven't worn a shirt with buttons in one million years.

I match my pace to theirs and know Jane will be annoyed if I walk next to her and let her notice me as a surprise. Instead, I touch her shoulder, with two fingers, as if we are only friends.

"I'm here," I say. And she bites off a word and turns to me, and she's flushed with the day and the walk and the conversation, absorbed in them, as she can be, and she's surprised and there's a moment when I know that I've again done something wrong, but I haven't. She stops where she is and wraps me in a full body hug, knocking her teeth into my shoulder. She's sweating, and smells like herself.

"You came!" she says.

"I called out at work. I'm very, very sick," I say, and nod over her shoulder at the young, bearded stork-man, and he smiles and raises his eyebrows in shared acknowledgment of what I don't know; he has bright blue eyes I could imagine girls talking about. An old woman talking to her friend knocks into us and Jane steps on my foot and the woman says "Sorry, dear!" and continues on.

"We can keep going," I say and Jane is already continuing, releasing and locking her hand around my elbow.

"This is the biggest crowd so far," she says.

"It's something," I say.

"Tuesday's was a little bigger," says the blue-eyed stork.

"You think?" says Jane.

"The important thing is we're here," he says.

"I hope Denise has the Channel 9 on in her basement right now," she says.

"Not while her stories are on," he says. I have no idea what they're talking about. An inside joke.

"I just heard from Denise," I say.

"Yeah?" says Jane, used to me.

"The squirrels came back," I say. "She can hear them in the walls."

"You know Denise?" says the blue-eyed stork. "From the principal's office?"

"No," says Jane. "I'm sorry. Matt, this is Doug. He teaches seventh-grade history—you know." I didn't know.

"Sure," I say.

"You remember. That conference in Tulsa." I didn't remember.

"Doug," I say, offer my hand to him, and he takes it. His hand is big and sweaty and soft and strong.

"Good to meet you finally," he says. Finally? I think.

"You too," I say and squeeze his hand back with what I hope is a non-aggressive but also insistent amount of pressure.

"What's the plan?" I say, to Jane.

Doug says: "We're going to head into the rotunda in half an hour."

"There's a couple state senators who are gonna give speeches," says Jane with Christmas morning enthusiasm. "TV's already in there setting up. I talked to someone from 5, just now."

"You'll be good on TV," I say.

"It's happening," she says. "There's such a good energy."

"We can do anything if we stay together and stick to the plan," says Doug. "It's a great lesson for the kids." I want to punch him in the face.

"Doug has his whole gifted class here," says Jane brightly. "Did you see the kids out by the War Memorial? Handing out bottles of water?"

"Yup," I say. I hadn't.

"I'm glad you came," she says.

"You're up at the new Costco?" says Doug.

"Yup," I say.

"I love their muffins," he says.

"Everyone does," I say.

"Are you gonna come in with us?" she says.

"I'm going wherever you're going," I say. I mean it to be more sentimental and direct than what I usually say, but it comes out like everything else I say. "I mean it," I say, and I do. Being in the march is making me feel oddly stretched-out, and I'm about to explain this badly but Jane is looking past me, into the street we're now walking next to. There's a black SUV, not brand new, drifting down Lincoln alongside us, in the lane closest to the

27

sidewalk, windows rolled down. A dude in the passenger seat is leaning out of the window—a guy like my dad's boss, puffy clean-shaven white face, white dress shirt, some kind of ID card on a lanyard around his neck. He's talking to someone walking in front of us; I hear his voice, higher-pitched than I would have guessed: "Fat and lazy!" he says, and something else, then "I work all summer to pay for your damn days off!" A woman in front of us waves him away. And then Doug takes a step toward the street, awkwardly in Jane's path, and she grabs onto me and halts and I grab onto her as if she's about to tip over, though of course she isn't.

"We're all working all summer, too!" says Doug.

"Bullshit!" says the dude.

"Stop," says Jane. The SUV is drifting toward us. The guy looks right at me. His eyes are wet like he's drunk, but there's no way he's drunk. He's not even really angry, I see; he's enjoying himself. Still, what gets to me isn't him—basic asshole-desperation for attention is easy to tune out—it's the other dude, driving, another clean-shaven, fat-faced white guy in a white shirt with a lanyard, one hand on the wheel, not laughing but smirking, not even paying attention to the argument, even though Jane is standing right in front of him.

"Such a butthead," I say to the dude driving and think, not a great line, but the dude leaning out of the window locks eyes on me.

"What did you say?" he says.

"Your face is a butt," I say, and he whaps his buddy the driver with one hand, barks "Stop the car!" and he opens the door and steps out awkwardly as the SUV stops, and he jerks into the door and is knocked back briefly into the seat. "Fuck," he says, gets his balance, comes toward me.

"Matt!" says Jane. I feel Doug pull her away from me.

"It's okay," I say. I keep my eye on office dude as he approaches. He's even younger than I assumed; maybe even my age. I feel paralyzed, like in a dream. The dude is shorter than it seemed like he was from the SUV window, but he has thick arms and shoulders—probably played high school football. He's standing too close to me, like he can't see well.

"Say that again, chickenshit," he says. He smells like a sandwich.

"That again chickenshit," I say of course. I don't even have the thought to get my hands up to protect my face until I'm already on the ground, my skull and ears and eyes buzzing and ringing. For a few seconds it's like being in the bottom of a giant aquarium: the churning of bodies above me. Red T-shirts come to my aid; one woman flails at the dude with a black purse. When I push myself up, the dude is already shedding the red T-shirts and making his way back into the SUV.

"You better run," I tell him and it comes out as a thick mumble, and the SUV pulls away into traffic with a screech, door flapping like a broken wing. I touch the numb someone-else's face that is the side of my face; from one of my eyes I see only a blurry sheet of tears. Then Jane is in front of me, holding all of my buzzing head in the heaven of her hands.

I'm found.

"What are you doing?" she says.

I'M watching *The Great British Bake Off* with a sandwich bag full of melting ice pressed to my eye socket when my sister Sylvie gets home from school.

"You try to kiss yourself in the mirror again?" she says.

"That's a complicated joke to come up with in one second," I say.

"I'm good like that," she says, then dumps her backpack covered in ball-point pen writing on the shoe shelf and heads into the kitchen.

"Aren't you going to ask me what happened?" I ask.

She rummages around in there, comes back with one of the Coors Lights.

"What?" she says, even though I'm not giving her a look because I guess she thinks I'm giving her a look. I used to perform being a punk jerk, too, but I actually was one.

"You're day drinking now?" I say.

"Whatever, Mom," she says. She's going to stomp off to her room, but she comes and sits on the couch next to me. She peels the wet bag off my head. "It's not that bad," she says. She takes a modest swig of the beer and presses the beer against the skin of my temple and takes my hand up to hold it there.

"So who'd you piss off?"

"Some guy who was getting mouthy at Jane."

"You were down at the teachers' protest?"

"I was."

"That's not your style. I'm impressed."

"Hell of a lot of good I did," I say. "Or anyone did, really. Nothing's going to change."

"It's just the first step," she says. She's excited, too, as she only is on the phone with the door closed. "Bodies in the streets. Mass action is the only true recourse we have as a class."

"As a class?" I say. "When did you turn into a commie?"

"I just don't think we should give up before we even try," she says.

"You honestly think it'll work then?"

"Nothing else has," she says. "How's Jane?"

"The same," I say. "You know."

"I have no idea what she sees in you," she says.

"I love you, too," I say.

"You know what I mean," she says, and I do. "Where's Mom?"

"The store," I say. That's why she'd snatched out the beer; rebel that she wants to be, she'd never risk such a thing if Mom's car was in the driveway.

"How's Rebecca?"

"Aunt Becky?"

"She says her friends all called her Rebecca."

"How should I know?"

"You're the only one home."

"The door's closed. Mom said she was sleeping and that I had to sit here and listen for her bell."

"Jesus, Matt," she says, then gets up. She creeps down the hall; I hear her open the door more quietly than she has ever opened a door in her life. On TV it is raining on a meadow of tiny yellow British flowers, then a woman is sliding a knife into a square of white sponge cake with impossible tenderness. The door closes more quietly than it was opened. The Coors Light is yanked away from my face. "She's sleeping," says my sister with the beer.

"That's what I said."

"But you didn't know." We watch on TV a woman in a long dark hijab squat to peer into an oven; outside the baker's tent there is a shimmering light rain in a green world.

"I wonder if I could get a job watching things bake," I say.

"You have to check on her," she says.

"What's the worst that could happen?" I say.

"Very funny," she says. I wasn't trying to be funny. "You have to check on her," she says.

"Okay, Mom," I say. She circles around the couch and stands over me, and for a moment it's like she's going to slap me. Then she sits down.

"You know she got arrested for chaining herself to a tree in Oregon?" she says.

"Dad told me she got caught trying to walk out of a JCPenney with a bunch of handbags jammed down her pants."

"That's not the whole story."

"That's all I know, really."

"Do you know anything about what happened with her and Dad?"

"Not much. What do you know?"

"Ask her." She passes me the beer. "I didn't really want this," she says, and turns to leave.

"You know," I say, "I really liked that song you were singing the other day. I like lots of your songs. I'm not saying that to be nice." I expect her to brush me off and drift away.

"Why?" she says, suddenly anchored.

"What do you mean? It's a good song."

"You always act like nothing matters, like nothing's going to change. But if you can appreciate a song you've never heard before, you believe that a better world is possible. Face it: you're a closet idealist."

"I'm drinking a Coors Light at 2 p.m. on a Wednesday," I say.

"You don't have to drink it if you don't want to," she says. "You're still on the hook for Rebecca's bell."

"I said I was," I say, and she disappears into the hall, the sanctuary of her room. I take a deep pull of the cold but skunked Coors Light and set it on the coffee table. I consider that I have no space in the house with a door to shut the rest of the world out. It's like never being able to close my eyes.

LATER, Connor is doing 110 out on I-40 past Weatherford, driving into and from vast darkness. The car is full of smoke sweet and green and sick as a million dollars floating in a bath. The hollow of one eye and down my cheek still feels mushy and fizzy. I'm not letting myself sink into the high as I always do; it is and isn't my choice. My eye waters; the world is a greasy window I can't wipe clear.

"I'm not gonna skip work tomorrow," I say between songs.

"You said that five times already," says Connor.

"I did?"

"We're here." He turns on silence. There's nothing anywhere.

"Where's here?" I say as in the distance I see alongside the highway a weak little mushroom of yellow light—the hovering sign for the Love's— and then there's the exit sign, and he tilts us off the highway onto the ramp, still flying. The stop sign is also flying, toward us, and beyond it is more nothing. I don't say anything. Too late, Connor leans onto the brake and the world grinds slower, aching, and I'm pulled forward by gravity until the car yanks me back to a whole halt. I can feel the weight of my sloshing, swollen, tender brain.

"Good grip. You get what you pay for," says Connor, satisfied. I blink and blink, but the hurt in my skull doesn't dissolve.

We park at Love's. I'm on my way in for what I'm not sure yet—a Mountain Dew and a bag of fire cashews—but Connor is walking across the McDonald's drive-thru lane toward where the semis are parked. They are larger in real life than in imagination or when passing them on the highway, old giants in wizard's caps, sleeping in rows. The smell of mysterious wet rust. We are one step away from climbing up into the cab of one that Connor somehow has acquired the keys for; we rumble it to life, ease onto the highway, aiming due North toward a glittering new isolated Arctic life. I wonder what it would be to simply drive away from home. How does one of these hulks get itself over a mountain? How does even a car engine work?

Connor keeps on past the trucks. He's taken off his suit coat and tie and has left them in the car. At the end of the parking lot, there's an empty standing hood where a pay phone used to be, a curb—then empty land, bristled with grasses and dead grasses, flat as a sea, out into the dark. Connor steps confidently over the curb and starts to run. He moves like a glitching video game, bent oddly to one side, his legs jerking in hitching but functional rhythm. It's easy enough to keep up, and then gain on him. Soon it's so dark I can only see the vaguest outline of his darkness in the larger darkness. The earth below my feet is soft, like a stomach, like something used to be grown here. I follow his thumping feet and hear his wild breathing. He's pitched forward, hands on his knees. I get close enough to touch him and he takes off again. When we stop, we're swallowed in the dark. He flops backwards, as into a pool. I sit next to him. Inside my face hurts. I don't feel like looking up at the stars. I look back at the human world of the Love's and its parking lot, yellow-light snow globe far away in the Oklahoma night.

"Is this for poetry?" I ask him.

"Everything is for poetry," he says. "Think how much you would pay for this, if you couldn't just go see it whenever you wanted." I give in. I tip my head back to look up. I close my hurt eye to see better. Stars to me have always made me think of brilliant bits of sand sparkling after a receding wave. I don't know what to do with this resemblance. I can't help feeling there is another wave coming.

"I have been to the ocean four times," I say.

"I'm going to call the poem 'Money and Energy,'" Connor says. He doesn't sound manic, like at lunch when he calls me and someone else calls him on some other phone, and he tells me to hang on and he tells the other phone to hang on and he talks to someone else. Now he sounds like a little kid.

"Okay," I say.

"If you look up long enough without letting your eyes focus, you can begin to sense patterns."

I open my watery eye and try. There are too many stars.

"Everything is blurry," I say.

"The error is in you," he says. "Ask yourself: why is everything blurry?"

"I told you. I got punched in the face."

"I know. But why did you let yourself get punched in the face?"

"The guy was yelling at Jane."

"I know what happened. I'm asking you why you let it happen."

"I didn't try to get punched."

"Of course you did. Every action has consequences, right?"

"But what you want to happen isn't always what happens."

"I'm talking about purpose. Not wishes and hopes."

"Okay."

"You can't just want. You have to line up purpose and consequences ahead of time and then follow through—that's what works, that's why stars work. That's energy and pattern. That's money. That's the world. That's the poem."

I consider infinity.

"So you think I should have punched him first," I say.

"You shouldn't have been there at all," he says, "without a plan for positive, effective action."

"Jane was glad I was there," I say. At first.

"But what you did there is more important than presence. And what you did was let yourself get punched in the face."

"I can still see," I say. "Mostly."

"You should come work for me," he says again. The idea is like a tree walking.

"I can't."

"Why not?"

"Because."

"Listen to yourself," he says. I do. I close the wounded eye, and the good worthless eye. I hear the sound of wind moving over the face of the sea of the earth.

Thursday

I OPEN MY eyes and see the face of a stranger. A woman younger than my mother all in sky blue stands in the center of the living room rubbing lotion on her hands, down to her wrists, with professional ardor.

"Mr. Matt, you're gonna let the day get away from you," she says. She notices my face, the bruise. She cocks her head. "You've been putting some ice on that eye?" I touch my eye socket: numb and tender, but my identifiable face again.

"I will," I say, and then, "I work at noon." I find I'm not embarrassed, or worried. She seems to find the whole situation absolutely normal. I see she's some kind of visiting nurse.

"I had hours like that before," she says. "Never got used to walking out of a big bright store into the dark."

"You like your job now better?"

"I do."

"How's she doing?"

"She's awake. You should go in."

"I have to get to work."

"Mmhmm. You looking after your mother?"

"Oh. No—that's my aunt. Aunt Becky."

"I know. I mean your mother," she says. I consider. "It's hard to be the main caregiver, even if you go into it with your eyes open."

"I will," I say.

"There's no map for any of this," she says. "Even for me, and I'm in and out of houses like this all day long."

"What's this house like?"

"It's a normal house," she says. "It's a nice house. And there's a person dying inside it." I suddenly feel like I have been inhospitable.

"Do you want a waffle?" I say. "I usually make some waffles."

"I'm on the clock," she says.

"Me too," I say. She smiles, as if she understands how I can't help agreeing with people I'm talking to, and at inappropriate moments.

"I'm Sheila. I'll be around."

"I'm Matt. You know that already."

"I do."

I AM too relieved to find a text from Jane. But it says, *We need to talk*.

About what? I say. No response.

Dolphin emoji, I say. No response.

I SHOWER, gulp five ibuprofen, and am on my way out the door to work when I turn around and make myself go look into my room—Aunt Becky's room. In there the TV is murmuring about spun sugar in a British accent; Aunt Becky is also a watcher of *The Great British Bake Off*. She's pale, but sitting up, hands folded placidly in her lap, sheet tucked tightly around her body. My old bed frame and mattress have been removed—I can't imagine how or when or where or by whom. The only house I've ever lived in is the permanent structure of my imagination, but it's not permanent in real life; it's like colors suddenly have different names. On the other side of the room now is a chair of unknown history, a thin flower-cushioned recliner that could be patio furniture. My mother sits in it, not watching TV but reading one of her bright-lettered detective novel paperbacks I'm sure she has already read. There's a stack of books and a Diet Sprite can on the carpet at her side.

"You off?" says my mother, glancing up over the top of the book, as if everything is normal. I consider what Sheila would want me to do. I consider Jane.

"You need anything?" I say.

"You're offering?" She's too surprised.

"I'm standing here saying these words."

"I may text you about some groceries later."

"Aunt Becky?" I say. She is watching TV with a slight frown and I think she didn't hear me, but then a cake is slid into an oven across the ocean and she looks up at me, pain-killer foggy. "Do you need anything?" I ask.

"You have a spare liver?" she says.

"I have an employee discount at Costco."

"A case of champagne."

"Matt," says my mother, as if I said it.

"The chocolate muffins are really good," I say.

"Chocolate muffins," says Aunt Becky.

AT Costco, I park far out like I'm required to, and there in a far corner all by itself, is a clean little white Toyota: Jane's car.

She gets out as I pull in; her bright red T-shirt is tucked with a forceful neatness I will never possess into the carnation-pink jeans she was wearing when I met her. When I get out of the car, she takes a few too-purposeful steps toward me—she's got something terrible to say—but when she gets closer, she sees my bruises and her face softens. She touches with two fingertips, light as a dragonfly, the unharmed skin of my cheekbone, on the edge of the tenderness.

"Look at your face," she says.

"I can't exactly do that right now," I say.

"I can't believe you did that," she says. "It was so stupid."

"I was trying to protect you," I say. She takes her hand back; I've said the wrong thing.

"I've been putting everything I have into teaching for the past year," she says, "and then into this protest. My boyfriend shows up and five minutes later I have to see him get punched. How's that protecting me?"

"He was an asshole," I say.

"The whole world is full of assholes!" she says. "That's why we were there! The whole point is to get them to listen to us, not to start stupid fights!"

"It's not gonna matter," I can't stop myself from saying. Her shoulders stiffen.

"Do you really believe that?"

"No," I say and hear myself.

"Right," she says, blows out a breath. "Maybe we're just moving in different directions."

"I'm only trying to be realistic."

"I have to go."

"You can stay a minute."

"You've got work," she says. And she goes.

I'm stuck in place like a lightning rod.

I tell myself I will know what to say when she rolls down her window to say goodbye.

But she doesn't roll down the window. And then she's gone.

"I do have work," I say to no one. It's the angriest thing I have ever said.

I walk into work like a balloon full of sand. Boss Jessica spots my black eye from a distance and is delighted. She says, "I hope you didn't put a steak on that. I once gave myself an eye infection!"

"Just ice," I manage.

"What happened to you?"

"I lost a fight to a clown."

"Happens to the best of us." Small misfortunes make Boss Jessica more insistently cheerful. The only thing I really know about her life is that her oldest son died in Iraq—I think in a helicopter crash.

She directs me to open 4, with the sticky drawer.

"You've got purple marker on your cheek," I tell her.

"You think I don't know that?" she says, doesn't bother to even pretend to wipe it away.

As soon as I count in and get on, it's busy enough to distract away pain and worry. The day goes. It's not like I ever feel like I'm accomplishing anything, but I can enter a state of blank functionality, like how it must feel to be a key.

Boss Jessica sends Jaden over to box up orders for me. He's twenty and looks like a melting cop. He works hard. When it's slow, he drives me crazy because he can't stand still—he's got to empty the register trash, replace the stock of refill tape, spray-and-wipe the belt, sweep the aisle. He'll ask what I'm going to do that weekend and when I tell him something about the movies or overtime he'll say *uh-huh, I'm going down four-wheeling with Ricky*. He's selling one or buying one or fixing one or getting one fixed. He came in one Monday with a giant bandage wrapped around a forearm. In a dead moment, he peeled it open, pointed the streak of torn-open flesh toward me, and only then asked, "Wanna see?" When it's busy, he doesn't make chit-chat but concentrates on stacking the cereal and batteries and frozen chicken breasts as efficiently and in as few boxes as possible. He whips items out of my hands as I pass them down after waving them through the scanner; I try to keep up; I try to get ahead, trust my fingers and memory to fire in produce codes without looking. At one point, I number in jalapeños as watermelons and realize afterwards, but don't fix it because in the instant I allow myself to appreciate it: the idea of a jalapeño-sized-watermelon and watermelon-sized-jalapeño seems correct.

After a while, it calms down, and Boss Jessica comes over and flicks off the 4 while I've got my hands full with bottles of vitamins for a too-ma-ny-cigarettes grandma. A watchful-toddler part of my soul always resents when my light is turned off for me. She sends Jaden to restack a pallet of tipped-over Tic-Tac packs.

"Carts," says Boss Jessica, to me. "Then you gotta take your lunch."

"Aye aye," I say.

OUT in the parking lot, I see Connor has texted me a photograph of a palmful of loose diamonds the size of drops of water—no words. I don't reply. I collect carts.

I gulp four ibuprofen and don't take my lunch.

AFTER work, I drive to Connor's. He lives in Deep Deuce, what used to be an old black neighborhood before it got wiped out for the highway, a fact I don't remember learning but somehow know. Now it is fertile ground for expanding condo complexes full of other people my age who work in oil and gas and money—young women with shampoo-commercial hair, young men in gray polos so soft and shiny they are almost silver—people I never would have been friends with in college. Connor, to be fair, is not friends with them either, though they share a genre of knowledge. Connor said once they want to make money work for them, and he wants to be the way money works. The condos have facades of elegantly sandpapered spaceship with too many, too few, too-narrow, or too-wide windows. The accent colors are muted but somehow hip, swampy greens and pollution blues and headache-bright browns. They sit atop drive-in garages protected from ordinary people by keycard access. I park in the street and duck around the restricting arm to walk into the garage where the sign says I am not allowed because I am a person. Connor is not supposed to let me have a resident elevator key or the code, but I have the key and I have the code.

The carpet of the hallways is luxurious and alien, as if the pattern of an oriental rug was tugged out of human looping curves into bad-dream infinite lines. The walls smell like expensive soap. The lamps set into the wall are brass snails emerging from radioactive milk with their eyes burning.

I knock on Connor's door, even though he never answers, even though every time after I use the key and go in and say, *didn't you hear me knock*, he says, *I know you have the key, you know, so when I hear someone knocking I know it can't be you. But it's me*, I say. *You have a key*, he says.

I knock again. He doesn't answer the door. I use the key.

Inside it's dark. There's a rumbling, whistling sound at first, like we are underneath a subway, or there is a tornado gathering outside in what

I had thought was a calm night, but then there is a scatter of violins screeching and some deep clunking of timpanis, and he's listening to avant-garde classical music again. The violins screech and the timpanis clunk again in exactly the same way, and again, a repeated figure full of nonsense and secrets; a piano enters, wanders within the pattern, and complains. (Connor has never seen Dream Nerve play. "I don't see the appeal of drowning the mind in an ocean of noise," he said, and I wished I was drowning my mind in an ocean of noise, chiming obliterating noise.) Connor's apartment is large and sparsely furnished. The main living space is split—one half is ordinary pretentious-rich-young-male apartment—leather couch, enormous flat TV for when I can convince him to sit still and watch a basketball game and eat something. I find Connor on the other side in what he calls his brain room—a corner desk, five monitors, two keyboards, a music stand with nothing on it. All the monitors are on; one is scrolling wildly up through a million rows of names and numbers. Another is on a live feed of a bald eagle in a nest, whited out in night-vision, asleep.

He doesn't turn.

"Hey," I say.

"I'm into the vein now," he says. "I'm being pulled into the heart of the world."

"What's open," I say. "Tokyo?"

"Time doesn't matter at the moment," he says.

I leave. There's no point in going to sleep since I don't have work tomorrow. As if there is ever a point to going to sleep, or a point to waking up.

I text Jane, *hey*. I text Jane, *sorry*. Nothing.

DRIVING in the gray grid of Oklahoma City late is like being a single photon of light, gliding frictionless from wire to wire to wire.

WHEN I get home, there is a baseball game on TV on mute, from Seattle (I can tell by the particular dampness of the dark-green grass against the gray-blue of the uniforms) and my father sits in a corner of the couch, head

41

tilted slightly to the right and leaning into the arm. I know his eyes are mostly closed. He's the kind of more-or-less asleep he only gets when he's very drunk, which is rare. If I were to wake him up, he'd be insanely angry about something I didn't do. There are many beer cans on the coffee table—cans of beer I brought home for Aunt Becky among them. He only ever leaves beer cans on the coffee table and watches TV late at night to make a point in an argument with my mother that I don't understand.

I'm surprised to see Sylvie is also in the room. She's asleep in the recliner, long night shirt, curled up like a child under a blanket, but she isn't under a blanket. Her shins are bare and I can see they are scratched up, like she's been running through pricker bushes. My looking at her wakes her up. She blinks, regards me as if I am a slight change in the weather. She glances to check my father's face, then leans forward to the TV remote and flicks the channel.

In the night, everything is on fire. There's an unstuck, vibrating quality to the image on-screen—perhaps a helicopter hovering and tilting down to look over the face of a hill. It's almost abstract: fractal patterns of oranges flickering into reds, tendrils sparking into pools of surrounding darkness. Streams of pure energy, of a piece with what Connor thinks he can sense and use, the paths of least resistance followed by electricity and streaming numbers, money and the dream of frictionless money. Sylvie ticks the sound up one. I can't really hear from across the room, but the news-anchor voices are murmuring and flat like always, like nothing is wrong. The shot switches to what at first is a line of trees against the sunset, but the sunset is bleeding through the trees; the sunset is a wall of flame.

A jerk then into daylight, the human world. A road through a forest of charcoal-blackened not-trees. I think of teeth pulled out of their sockets. A little white car like Jane's car looks like a human skeleton heat-warped, crumpled, melted into asphalt.

"That's California, right?" I say. The banner at the bottom of the TV says, "Wildfires in California." My sister doesn't bother answering. My father stirs but doesn't wake. "Why are you watching fires on the news?"

"They stopped getting rain," she says. "Like, totally. For months. Worst drought in a hundred years. It's not far from Fresno. There's a town that's totally cut off."

"What do you care about Fresno?" I say. She doesn't answer. On TV a man with perfect hair stands against distant swirls of fire in a gleaming yellow raincoat.

"This is going to happen more and more," says Sylvie.

"It's not like we can do anything about it," I say.

"Cool," she says. "Good attitude."

"I'm just saying. It's all going to shit."

"At least you admit there's something wrong. That's more than I can say for some people."

"I think Jane is breaking up with me," I say out loud for the first time. And she looks up, and she's going to say something cutting, and I'm ready to get it over with.

"She is?" says Sylvie, wincing. "She didn't say."

"You talk to Jane?"

"We text sometimes."

"It's for the best, I guess," I say. "For her." Sylvie turns back to the fire.

"I don't know about that," she says. It's the nicest thing she's ever said to me. "But whatever happened, it's your fault. Figure out how to get her back. You have to try. I bet that's what she needs. For you to not just give up." She's still watching the fire on TV like it's watching her.

The front door opens behind me in a burst; I twist to defend myself.

It's somehow my mother. She's got her hair back like she does when she's working in the yard and is already tearing off her shoes. She's never out this time of night.

"Where were you?" I say.

"Church," says my sister, still watching the news.

"Why were you at church?" I say. My mother is about to snap at me, but she catches herself, smooths her face down with one hand.

"I needed a moment of peace; is that so much to ask?"

"No," I say.

"No," she says, not angry. Even I could understand the appeal of a church in the evening with no one else inside of it.

"Rebecca's been asleep the whole time," says Sylvie. My mother doesn't respond but walks through the room, through us, to the hallway to check on Aunt Becky.

I turn back to the TV. The next story is the ongoing teacher protests. There's a shot of the red-T-shirted teachers at the Capitol taken from a helicopter the same height as the helicopter over the fires. Somewhere in that sea of red-T-shirted people is Jane.

Then I see, in a line on the sidewalk, a dozen uniforms—cops.

"Why's there so many police there?" I say to the TV.

"Someone said a guy driving by was waving around a gun."

"How did you know that?"

"It's possible to know things."

The TV flicks to a commercial for, it seems at first, the ocean.

"I don't like the idea of Jane being there if it's not safe," I say.

"Nowhere's safe," says my sister.

"Everyone's home," says my father, without raising his head or opening his eyes.

"We are," I say.

Friday

I WAKE UP on the floor at the foot of the couch with a blanket covering me that I didn't cover myself with. There's microwave-beeping and cabinet-opening noise in the kitchen. By the light in the room, it's ten. The beer cans have been cleared away from the coffee table. I remember waking up on weekends and hearing my parents move through the house as I pretended to still be asleep; I remember feeling protected. Now I feel naked.

I scoot myself forward on my elbows and peer around the corner into the kitchen. It's Aunt Becky. As if she is floating an inch above the floor. She's wearing what I recognize as my mother's robe, a too-long lavender cloud that had been presented to her wrapped in shimmering silver paper with great ceremony by my father for her birthday. Aunt Becky is staring into the counter, into a mug dotted with little blue flowers that I have never seen before.

I pull myself to my feet and make my way into the kitchen. I notice she's holding on to the lip of the counter with one hand; the other hand is laid on its side on the counter like she can't hold it up. Her hand is thin, and I can see the veins and the bones.

"Are you okay?" I say.

She says, "I'm waiting for the tea to steep," without looking up.

"You want me to do it?"

"No." She watches. I inch forward to see, too. There's a raspberry red blooming in the water, just too-bright and close-to-purple to be blood. I touch the side of the mug with two fingers—it's only warm.

"You want it heated up?" I say.

"I can't have it too hot," she says. "I don't really like tea, anyway. I'm doing it for the process."

"I get it," I say. "I like to stare at microwave popcorn."

"Freak," she says, gazing into the mug. Actually, watching the outward progress of the color in the water is interesting. I think of jellyfish, soundwaves from whispers.

"I guess you can get around pretty good," I say.

"I'm unsteady," she says, flatly, without complaint. "I should lie down."

"I'll bring you back to your room," I say. She doesn't move. I realize I have no idea how to help her walk. Briefly I consider that I should lift her up like a bride. "Should I just take your hand, or," I say, and she moves the hand that had been locked on the counter onto my forearm. I lift my arm out toward her, holding it parallel to the floor; she grips and presses down.

"I can walk like this," she says, angry, as if I'd implied she couldn't. She looks in my face. Her eyes are wet and spidered with blood vessels. I can't not smell piss.

"Okay," I say.

We make our way out of the kitchen into the hall.

"I'll come back for your tea," I say.

"I don't want it." Her grip is not strong, but it's serious. The door to her room is open. My mother is in the same clothes from yesterday, leaning back in the chair, a sweatshirt opened and laid across her crossed arms, her mouth wide open. I can't remember ever having seen her asleep. I can hear the catch in her breathing—she's got a bit of a cold.

"Ma," I say, and she comes to.

"What?" she says. "What are you?" and she's hauling herself to her feet.

"It's alright," I say. "You should go to bed."

"What time is it?" she says, then comes to us at the door, one hand out, hovering, under Aunt Becky's wrist.

"I'm not made of glass," says Aunt Becky. She shakes off my arm and takes a step past my mother into the room, struggles like an uncertain swimmer through the few feet of air to the edge of her bed, rests her hands there, takes a breath. "I'll need help getting up."

"Of course," says my mother, at her side instantly. She snaps her head back to look at me. "You know, it's really irresponsible of you to get your aunt out of bed without asking me first."

"It wasn't my idea," I say. I expect Aunt Becky to take my side, but I see her knee is trembling. I get to her as it starts to give way.

"Shit legs," she says.

"Let's get you back in bed," says my mother.

"I've got you," I say. "Hold her head steady," I say to my mother, and I crouch and get an arm under her knees, and another under her shoulders, and I lift her up, like I knew I should have, like a bride.

She's heavier than I expected, which I suppose is good.

I lay her down, trying not to break the surface tension of the lake of the bed. I've never tried to be so gentle before.

"That hurts," says Aunt Becky. I realize my face doesn't hurt anymore. She holds one arm at an angle, like it's stuck in a cramp.

My mother shoulders me out of the way. She has a pill pinched between two fingers like she just plucked it from a flower; she dips to Becky, slips the pill into the corner of her mouth, and whacks me with her other hand.

"Water," she says. I grab the flowered tumbler from the side table and pass it to my mother, who holds it to Becky's lips with a firm, impersonal, ceremonial air, as if it was communion wine. Growing up, she was the only one of the family to take the communion wine at Mass; she is the only one of us who still always goes.

When Aunt Becky swallows, it's like she has to think the action of each muscle in her throat. Through the process, my mother holds the water close to Aunt Becky's mouth in readiness. Aunt Becky doesn't say she doesn't want another sip of water; she closes her mouth. She closes her eyes. My mother puts her hand on her shoulder.

Slowly, Aunt Becky's cramped hand drifts slack, toward the bed, as if she is releasing a heavy weight moment by moment.

"I just want to rest," she says so quietly it's like I imagine hearing her.

In the kitchen I tell my mother *I can sit with Aunt Becky if you want to get some rest or get out of the house, I can stay, it's my day off*, and she says, *I already slept half the damn day away. Why didn't you wake me up?* I tell her I was asleep and she says, *whose fault is that?* Her face is hard. *Fine*, I say. *Fine.*

There is still no text from Jane.

I am relieved when Simon presses his nose to my ankle, needing me. I take him for a walk so long he plops himself panting in a patch of shade under a distant neighbor's overgrown willow, and I have to pick him up and carry him home.

When I get back into the house, there's a new moaning. I almost leave. I realize it's not Aunt Becky. "I can't," says my mother. "I can't." I almost leave.

I stand in the doorway to Aunt Becky's room, and I see that Sheila the nurse has arrived. She's at the foot of the bed, holding one of Aunt Becky's feet up by the ankle, hand held slightly open to allow for Aunt Becky's squirming. Aunt Becky's eyes and mouth are pinched closed; it's like a parody of a parent tickling a child at first, but then I see on Aunt Becky's heel the wound—quarter-sized, raw flesh.

I see all at once that my mother's historical lack of sympathy or solicitude for nosebleeds and scraped knees was not a way to toughen us up, but a way to hide fear. She's white-faced, turned away from the bed, hand over her mouth.

"Young Matt," says Sheila calmly, her back still to me.

"Yo," I say.

"I need your help."

"Okay."

"Come around here," she says. I do.

"Help me keep her still," she says. I'm about to say, *how?*, but she says to Aunt Becky, "It's almost over."

I rest one hand on Aunt Becky's forearm—sticks wrapped in cloth—and I don't know what to do with my other hand, so I float it over her scalp and she turns slightly toward my almost-touch, like she's wondering who I am, and then Sheila says, "Done," and I look, and the bandage is applied, neat as a stamp.

"There now," says Sheila. Aunt Becky's looking at me.

"Monster," she says.

I GET out of the house into the city with nowhere to go and then, like the answer to a question in a dream, I see I'm going to the protest at the Capitol. I call Connor to tell him about Jane and to ask him if it would be insane to go to the protest at the Capitol to see her, and he says yes and to pick him up first because his car is being refreshed. I don't feel like asking him what that means.

He's standing on his new-sidewalked corner waiting for me in jeans and, somehow, one of the red teacher T-shirts. He's talking to the air. I know he's got his ostentatiously subtle silver earpiece in. He slips into the passenger seat mid-sentence like I'm his driver, which I am.

"...of other people's timelines," he says. "They don't mean anything except as a field of discussion. Right. Right. No."

"Hey, genius," I say.

"We're setting the terms," he says to the world. "If you get confused, say nothing. Okay. Yes. Good. I'm out." He reaches to lift his sunglasses from his eyes and he's not wearing any. He sets the nothing on the top of his head. "There's two ways to work the numbers," he says to me. "There's *ride the deep philosophy*, and there's *identify and perform the simple available action*. Anything else is anxiety and failure."

"I don't even know what the simple available actions are."

"I know. That's why you should work for me. You could learn as much as you want to. You could go as far as you want."

"I have a job."

"You keep saying that word, but I don't think it means what you think it means."

"Where'd you get the shirt?"

"It's a T-shirt," he says. "Not a magic sword."

"Do you even want the teachers to win?"

"Of course. That's why I'm wearing the T-shirt. The simple available action."

"It doesn't bother you that, like, they want to put more taxes on bank accounts or whatever?"

"Should a fish worry about the ocean?" he says. I consider.

"A dolphin could," I say.

"Let's face the matter at hand. Why did Jane break up with you?"

"She didn't say that exactly."

"Listen to yourself."

"She thinks we're living in different worlds."

"And you agree?"

"She has a point."

"Because there's only one world. Everything is connected. It's your job to understand how it's connected."

"Simple."

"What are you going to say when you see her?"

"We're not going to see her," I say. "It was totally random that I found her the other day. There's, like, a billion people there. She's probably inside talking to her senator or whatever. There's some voting on a spending bill this afternoon." I'm pleased with myself for discovering this detail from probably the news last night in the front of my brain. "And that's not why we're going anyway. We're going because it's the right thing to do."

"Because that's what Jane would do."

"Well, yeah."

"You're going to find Jane—say it out loud."

"No."

"Saying something out loud can make it true," he says, waits. I consider.

He seems to notice for the first time that he is in my car. He presses his fingerprint into the dashboard, then removes it and inspects it. "This car is too old," he says. He presses a button in his ear. "Give it to me," he says.

WE have to park even farther away from the Capitol than I did last time. There are no ruins on this street. There's a house with a neat, new green patch of lawn and an enormous OU flag next to the front door, as if the football team is a country, and on the corner there's a house in a cage of scaffolds—siding torn off and in the process of being replaced, a goggled man on the front walk with a table saw and a pile of lumber, a ladder leaning on a white van out front, a *For Sale* sign pressed into the dirt, "Under Contract" on top. I wonder who lived there; I wonder who is going to live there.

Connor considers the sign, arrives at an insight that is more like a resolution: "A house is a particular kind of number," he says.

"A house is years and years of a family's life," I say.

"Think about the city the way God would see it."

"I don't believe in God."

"It's an exercise!" he says, halts our progress with an arm barred across my chest. "It has explanatory power!" He closes his eyes. I keep mine open. "Imagine. You are an all-encompassing and sensing abstract intelligence intimately intrinsic in all things. The years are like hours. The houses rise and fall, whole neighborhoods. Forests move, too. Even mountains. It's all waves of energy, just at different scales." He opens his eyes. "So there is an equation that exists that describes the motion of the universe from God's perspective."

"What's the equation for that squirrel on the powerline?" I say, but he's only paying attention to ideas whirling around in his head. Once, in college, we got separated in a Target and I eventually found him cross-legged in an empty space of the paper towels shelf staring into the middle distance. When I touched his shoulder, he looked up at me and said, "How do we decide what food is?" The other kids on our hall in the dorm didn't know what to do with him; neither did I, but I was better at it.

We turn the corner and can see the nodding oil pump, lonely as a heron, and beyond, the blur of the red-T-shirted crowd, the Capitol overlooking the crowd not unlike Connor's God-perspective.

"Impressive!" he says with a pure, disinterested enthusiasm, the same way he received the night sky over Nowhere, Oklahoma. Neither makes him even a little bit quiet, or afraid. We are different. "This is perfect for the poem," he says.

"I'm not even going to look for Jane," I say.

"I've got an idea," he says, fiddling with his phone. "Why don't you look for Jane? I'm gonna collect some voices." He slides his phone back into his pocket.

"You have to ask for permission, right?" I say.

"A voice is in the air," he says. "You can collect as much air as you can hold."

"Maybe you should invest."

"I've thought about it."

When we get to the Capitol, it looks the same as it was: the tailgate tents shading frowning, visored geometry teachers on lawn chairs and roller-coolers full of Cokes and bottles of water. The parked school buses and charter buses with black windows lining the streets are the same; the tinny cheerful disco from loudspeakers is still the same, but the crowd is somewhat sparser—I was right about something important going on inside. Because I watched the story about yesterday's incident with the gun on the news, and only because I watched the story, I notice a few actual cops are arranged in a constellation around the open space. They are relaxed, but too watchful. I'm not comforted. There is still a circling march, but moving at a more leisurely pace.

"Jane's either inside," I say, "or she's marching."

"But you said you weren't looking for her," says Connor.

"Of course I'm looking for her," I say.

"Better to say it out loud," he says. We merge in. I look everywhere. Next to us is a woman with a sign hanging on her back, tied around her neck with what looks like a shoelace. In black stencil: "A Mind is a

Terrible Thing to Waste." She's sweating, fanning herself with a folded-up newspaper though the day is not yet hot. I try to match my pace to hers to stay behind, but Connor angles himself next to her.

"Great day for a march," he says.

"Could be worse," she says, fanning herself. "Could be stuck on the side of a highway in a storm. Could be walking through an earthquake."

"Is that so hard, really, if you're outside on flat land?"

"It's strange more than anything else," she says. "It's a little like sitting on a waterbed someone bumped into. That was about halfway from Tulsa."

"Fuck me," says Connor. "You walked from Tulsa?"

"Sure did," she says, "and be careful with your language. I'm still an English teacher."

"Are you listening?" says Connor, turning to me. "Anyone could walk across the state. Or the whole country. We're just so cognitively self-limited that we don't acknowledge the possibility."

"Well I don't know about all that," she says. "What I do know is that if I can do it, anyone can. I'd do anything for my kids."

"What grade do you teach?" he says.

"Eighth grade. Over in Broken Arrow. How about you?"

"Oh, I'm not a teacher. I'm just here to be here."

"Is that right?" she says.

"What's your favorite poem to teach?" he says.

"That's easy," she says. "'Stopping by Woods on a Snowy Evening.'"

"Snow!" he says. "I love it. Do you have it memorized?"

"I can't help having it memorized, by now."

"Can you recite it?"

"You want me to tell you a poem?"

"If you'd be so kind."

And she does, taking a break after every line to breathe. She keeps walking at the same pace. Connor listens loudly.

The poem doesn't make me imagine myself, or all of us, walking through a dark forest in the snow; it makes me imagine us walking on a sidewalk in Oklahoma City listening to a poem about the snow. I feel weirdly real.

She finishes.

"Nice," says Connor. He turns to me. "You should ask her if she knows where Jane's school is set up."

"I don't know what it's called," I say.

"How could you not know the name?"

"I know the place."

"How could you not know the name? The name is the place!"

"No, the place is the place."

"I wouldn't be able to help you anyway," says the teacher. "Everyone's everywhere."

"What's your estimate of the number of teachers here today?" says Connor.

"Oh, I don't know. A lot. I do wish the governor was here," she says. "I wish she could be down here with us so we could talk to her."

"What would you say?" I ask.

"I'd take her by the hand," she says. "I'd be gentle, but firm. I'd give her a piece of my mind."

Connor says: "I'd stand right in front of her and have us stare into each other's eyes for as long as we could without blinking."

"Dude," I say.

"What?" he says. "I'd do that with anyone."

WE continue marching inside the march.

There's a red-T-shirted woman in a wide straw hat sitting on a bench knitting something complicated and green. Connor plunks himself down next to her.

"So why are you here?" he says.

"Are you a reporter or something?" she says.

"I'm an apprentice capitalist poet," he says.

It turns out she teaches second grade. She has to buy her classroom's crayons. She also works weekends and some nights at Old Navy.

"That doesn't track as an ideal use of your energy," says Connor, thoughtfully. She gives him the look people give Connor.

We continue. Connor sidles up to strangers and makes conversation. I scan the crowd we are walking past, the crowd we are in, for Jane. In my looking, I lose Connor. Alone, looking into the crowd as hard as I can look, I see that the crowd is made of individuals. This thought strikes me as both stupid and profound. I see a teacher with one arm. I see a cop with biceps the size of my thighs. I see a teacher with a long black braid, thick as a snake. I see cheerful children and weary children also wearing the red T-shirt. I see a teacher with a neat gray beard and a fishing hat; it's my high school history teacher Mr. Mahoney. He is still too tall. He has his head tipped back, as if to read, and judge, the crowd ahead of him from under his glasses.

"Mr. Mahoney," I say, an eight-year-old reflex activated. I immediately regret speaking out loud. He turns to me, not surprised, as he never was, and studies me. It takes a moment, but then he smiles. His teeth are smoother and neater than they used to be; I suspect they are false teeth.

"I know your face," he says.

I tell him my name. He nods, still not there.

"What year?" he says. I tell him. He nods. "You're not a teacher," he says, and I don't like how sure he is, like maybe he does remember me and of course I could never be a teacher. I know I could never be a teacher, but I don't like the idea of someone else knowing it.

"No," I say. "But I wanted to be here." I don't say why. He nods.

"A significant moment in our history," he says. And I know what he's going to say. A pointed finger, a knuckle knocking on the corner of his desk: the power of democratic movements; the power of the people. On one wall of his classroom, he had an old Oklahoma state flag with the red and the star from the early twentieth century when it was apparently one of the most socialist places in the country. "Agrarian populism!" he would say in a too-many-cigarettes-raspy voice. It became a joke, something to bark in PE when whipping a dodgeball. He assigned five pages of his own typed, single-spaced material on labor unions in addition to the regular textbook reading. I didn't read it; in my defense, I didn't do the regular reading either.

I prepare to hear what I have heard before, as if I'm back stuck in that hot beige box of a classroom.

"I thought it was too late in the day," he says, oddly weakly. "But look at this." He opens one hand, and gestures generally outward, as if showing me a diagram he's drawn on the blackboard of the whole world. I notice his fingers are, slightly, trembling. He's older than I'd imagined.

I look past his fingers into the crowd and spot Jane in the distance. She's standing on the other side of the Capitol grounds, by the Native American woman statue, listening to someone at the mic on the makeshift stage who is for some reason waving around a pair of scissors. She's wearing a red bandana in her hair in a way she never has before.

"I gotta go," I say, and break through the stream to cross the crowd; Mr. Mahoney grabs my shoulder, and hard, with individual fingers. I look back. He lets go.

"Don't give up, okay?" he says, with absolute seriousness.

"Okay," I say, not meaning it and meaning it. I always say *okay*.

I'm walking across the face of the Capitol toward Jane when I see next to her bearded Doug, stiff as a mall mannequin; he is resting a finger on her shoulder and leaning in close to speak into her ear—too close— and she listens, and nods, professionally, maybe, and *what am I doing*. I stop where I am. I see they are in the middle of a long line—along the barriers that block off the stairs—that is making its way into a side door of the Capitol.

I join the back of the line. It moves steadily. Attached to a scaffold by zip ties is a laminated sign that says, "Excuse Our Appearance: Renovations in Progress. Oklahoma State Capitol Renewal Project, 2015."

The woman in front of me wears a baby in a sling. The baby has a face like a tiny old man with wet, perfect little black eyes that don't look at me like an animal doesn't look at me. I hope death is like being a baby. The baby's mother bounces gently from foot to foot; she listens to the woman next to her who is talking about what someone named Jackson will and won't eat. He loves green grapes. Right inside the doors is a metal detector, and the women tell the guard they are here to see Representative Pendleton. I tell the guard I am here to see Representative Pendleton. He nods. I put my wallet and keys on the belt to go through the X-ray. Inside the metal detector's invisible door through, I hear a tremendous beep, but it's not for me, and I am oddly disappointed.

I proceed around a corner into the scuffed white hallway of anywhere in America. A chubby lanyarded man in a suit hustles past me, a stack of loose pages flapping open in his hand like a bird he shot. I follow the slinged baby, but the baby turns after a sign that says "Stairs" and I continue on. Ahead of me is the conversational murmur of a mall at Christmas time without piped-in music; I enter a wider hallway and confront a wall-size painting of a forest and field at sunset. A confused adolescent deer looks at me and doesn't know how he got stuck in a painting any more than I know how I got myself into the state Capitol. Ahead of me I see at the end of the hall a school of fish of red T-shirts, and above them an opening out, as walking onto a beach.

I walk out into the rotunda. There is a general gleaming; it is the size and aura of a luxury cafeteria. Several stories above and extending further up is the dome itself, an elegant cellular pattern, a ring of windows around its interior allowing the diffuse brightness of sunlight through closed eyelids. Elsewhere above, murals of events, people, and symbols from history that are impressive and too far away to really see—wheat and grass, vague buffalo and men with long gray guns, a horse, a child, a river. Below, lanyarded men and women my age in professional clothes arrow here and there through the clumps of teachers on paths that no one else knows are there.

Above me, on the second-floor landing, a young man in a red T-shirt leans out over the railing. He's wearing a shirt and tie beneath his T-shirt. He has a very neat black beard.

"My fellow Oklahomans!" he calls. The teachers, a flock of squabbly flightless birds, pause and look up in one motion, like a well-behaved kindergarten class. I'm the new kid. "How are we feeling this morning?" he says. *How are we feeling*, I think to myself. Am I in the audience for a classic rock cover band? But the crowd on all sides roars its approval. A woman next to me is applauding badly, thumping the heels of her hands together, and I spot, through a split-second clearing in the crowd, Jane, and she's applauding correctly and looking up with all of her attention. Next to her, Doug has his hands jammed into his armpits for some reason and he's looking up, too, and nodding with what seems to me creepy enthusiasm.

"I don't know about y'all," says the speaker, sounding more like a news anchor than a country boy, "but I'm feeling . . . " he says, pauses, drawing it out, "Grrrrreeeeeat!"

The crowd applauds. A dude hoots into my ear.

"We're here representing our students!" he says. "We're here representing our communities from all across our great state! We're here from Tulsa!" he says to a responding general roar. "We're here from Elk City!" he says, to a smaller response, from near the back. "We're here from Guthrie!" he says, to a spatter of dying applause. "Where else?" he says. "Who else we got out there?"

"Duncan!" I hear. Something that has a lot of *o*'s in it. I spot through the crowd, again, Jane, leaning in to listen to Doug.

"Oklahoma City!" I say, much too loud, and too late to hear that the called-out names had petered out, so I'd screamed the name of the place we were all standing in into a pocket of quiet. A pencil-thin, crisp-new-khakis math teacher type standing in front of me turns to peer down at me, her unruly student. "Go Thunder!" I add, to her, and she twists her mouth, and I glance over to see that Jane has heard my voice. She isn't pleased. I can't think of anything else to say. "Sorry," I say silently through the crowd to her as the man on the balcony barks "Go Thunder!" and is answered by a pure and simple roar of the crowd that says only, "Here we are." I'm not part of it.

Above, the voice begins to talk about a session, and a bill, and today, and I'm moving toward Jane through the crowd that is parting for me too easily, as if they know I'm not one of them.

She's waiting for me.

"What?" is the only response I have for the way she's looking at me.

"What are you doing here?"

"Just trying to make up for the other day."

"By making an ass of yourself? This isn't a joke, you know."

"I know."

"You don't act like it. I'm supposed to meet our state rep now. Do you know who that is?"

"Yes," I say before I can think not to lie. She gives me a look.

"I have to go," she says, and she goes.

OUTSIDE I find Connor cross-legged in the grass on the way to the parking lot with a pack of science-fair-type teens playing Magic on a picnic blanket. He has a textbook open on his lap and is studying it deeply as if it is a sacred text.

"Yo," I say.

"This is their history textbook. It's from 1995!" he says to me, not looking up.

"That's public school," I say. "That's the way it is for us. That's why we're here."

"There's no 9/11! There's never going to be another war! It's a whole different universe!"

"We have to leave," I say.

"We're leaving," he says, reading.

IN the car I text and erase five separate, intricate apologies to Jane. When I get home, my father is standing on the front lawn in his socks, and my mother is standing in the open front door. There are many shoes scattered across the lawn where my mother must have thrown them. They don't turn to see the car as I park. They are facing each other. They've never done anything like this out in the world.

When I get out, it's clear they have just stopped screaming. They glare and wait for a cue from the audience to move them.

"What's going on?" I say. My mother is the first to break. She folds her arms across her chest, leans against the doorframe like a sheriff in a movie.

"Ask your father," she says.

"Don't tell him that," he says.

"I'm done," she says.

"Dad?" I say. He looks at me, then the shoes. They aren't only his shoes, I see. There's one of my mother's winter boots, my sister's old roller skates, a selection from the deep inventory of the hall closet. I could imagine how the shoe throwing, no matter how clearly motivated at first as an immediate, ironic rejoinder to whatever infuriating remark—"where did you hide my damn shoes!"—quickly lost its tight, purposeful symbolism and became an unstoppable tantrum. Also on the lawn is the neat, snapped-together navy travel umbrella we keep in the closet with the shoes. A pair of garden gloves, a magazine, the glow-in-the-dark frisbee. My father takes a deep breath and surveys the damage. He plucks up a beat-up sneaker.

"You only threw one of these," he says. My mother ducks back into the house and comes out with the other, and it's like she's going to throw it at him, but instead she walks down the step toward him, turns to me and tosses me the shoe. I don't bother reaching for it. She misses by ten feet and it thwacks into the side of my car.

"You can't take a step and reach out?" she says. "How many afternoons did I drive you to baseball?"

"Tell me you're gonna throw it to me next time," I say.

"You explain it to him," she says to my father, heading back to the house. I expect her to slam the door, but she does the opposite, closing it first quickly, then very slowly, softly. I hear the lock quietly but emphatically click into place.

My father is sitting in the grass, pulling on his one shoe. He looks uncomfortable, like his knees don't want to bend the way he is bending them. He holds out his hand for the other shoe.

"What's going on?" I say.

"Just give me my shoe," he says. I do. He frowns—the laces are tangled in a double knot. He sets the shoe in his lap and squints to his work.

"Dad," I say.

"Let's go to Buffalo Wild Wings," he says. "I need a drink."

"I could eat," I say. "Dad?"

"What?"

"What's going on?"

"I need a drink," he says.

"Should we clean up all this stuff?" I say. He looks out at the battlefield.

"I'll do it later." He squints into the shoe in his lap, works at the knot.

WE'RE sitting at a tall table against the wall. The restaurant is half full. The bartender is pulling a yellow beer and bouncing her head up and down like she's listening to music and not to the pure twangy announcer voice informing us gravely about the experimental adjustments a pitcher has made to his split-finger grip. There are one billion televisions in the room with us. Anywhere I look are baseball games and golf course expanses like luxurious green oceans. Then, multiples of a commercial for frozen meals that appear to be shot by a spacecraft orbiting a planet of macaroni and cheese that is studded with sharp red hunks of bacon. Connor would see some mystical implications. I see a shitload of macaroni and cheese. My father studies the Bible of the laminated menu like he's alone and it's important.

"Dad," I say.

The waitress arrives. She's my age, pretty, Jane-sized, with tight yellow-brown curls. She's chewing gum meditatively in a way I like. She smells like a shower. I make these observations as if from a great distance; she is not Jane. Her name tag says Samantha.

"Can I start you all with a drink?" Samantha says, to me.

"How do I order twelve wings?" says my father. She turns to him.

"We've got specials on ten and fifteen," she says. "You can order individually, but it's actually cheaper to just get the fifteen."

"I want twelve, and I want mild," he says, pointing at the menu with ridiculous urgency, like it's evidence. "Actually mild. Last time I couldn't finish."

"You got it," she says.

"Sorry, he just got out of surgery," I say.

"I know what that's like," she says, to me, and I know she's bullshitting and that she knows I'm bullshitting and that she knows I know she's bullshitting. "You want wings?" she says. I could tell her anything in the world.

"I'll have ten regular," I say, offering back the menu.

"You got it," she says, taking the menu and turning away, and my father raises his hand like probably one of Jane's students who knows the answer.

"And a Sam Adams," he says, still holding his hand up. "As big a bucket as you have back there."

"Two?" she says, to me.

"I'm only alive once," I say.

"So yes?" she says, not amused.

"Yes," I say. "Thank you."

She goes, and my father is again studying his menu, as if there is more to see.

"Dad," I say.

"What?" he says.

"Why are we here? What's the story?" He finally looks up.

"I don't talk about it," he says. "I don't like to even think about it. What your mother is doing with your aunt. I can't wrap my head around it."

"Dad," I say. "I have no idea what you're talking about." He considers.

"You know how much a new water heater costs?"

"Dad," I say.

"What do you think of her?" he says.

"Aunt Becky? She's alright."

"I'm serious."

"I don't know," I say. "It seems like she needs us."

"That's right," he says. "She does. What do you know about her life?"

"Just what you've told us. She's younger than you. She disappeared after high school and ended up in jail for a while, and you haven't talked in a long time."

"And what do you think about that?"

"I don't know," I say.

"You think we should help her."

"I guess so."

"There's so much you don't know. You just have no fucking idea." He says "fucking" the way he does, raising his voice slightly, biting it off. Growing up, it was his way of telling me to stop asking whatever I was asking for, to stop doing whatever I was doing. It used to work.

"Tell me, then," I say.

"That's what you want?"

"That's what I want," I say. I think he's going to snap again, but he doesn't. He looks away, sticks his tongue out the side of his mouth, as if to soothe the cracked corner of his lip. It's an unfamiliar gesture, but seems practiced, a kid's habit that got eliminated only through fierce concentration. He's thinking something over, and then there's a moment when he makes a choice.

"I want you to know how much I love your mother," he says, his voice not sad but exhausted. "This isn't about her."

"What does this have to do with Mom?"

"This isn't about her!" he says. A Bud Light bro glances over. I wait until he turns back to the baseball game.

"Okay," I say.

"Okay. So. Listen, okay? Listen all the way through."

"Okay," I say. And he takes a breath and looks away into the activity in the Buffalo Wild Wings. The bartender is clinking together a stack of pint glasses. A man is digging into something that looks like a brownie sundae poured onto a pizza with an enormous silver spoon. On many TVs, an Army commercial: identical soldiers climb identical jagged mountains of blue computer ice. My father looks at me.

"You know about my first girlfriend? Who died in a car crash?" he says.

"Yeah," I say. "Mom told me." It had been weird. I'd just gotten my license, was on my way out the door to smoke pencil-shavings-level pot in a garage with some other losers, and she grabbed me by the sleeve and said, "You're old enough to know," and then told me the story. I'd responded with a big performative *whatever*, though it did make me drive more carefully home that night, baked out of my face. She didn't want to talk anymore about it when I'd asked a few days later. And I'd never have asked my father.

"You don't know the whole story," he says.

"No," I say, and wait.

"Her name was Sylvia," he says. My sister's name.

"Oh," I say.

"I met her in college. She was from out past Tulsa, came down to OU on a partial academic scholarship. She was going to be a professor.

"She wasn't really the sort of girl I usually went for. I was a quiet kid. Now, I had friends. But I was quiet. I mostly kept my head down. I'm still not totally sure what she saw in me. I guess you never know the answer to that question, not really. But I'm glad I knew her. I had to be brave to be around her. To make my intentions known, they used to say. But I was brave. She made me brave," he says, runs his tongue into the crack of his lip. "Without knowing her, I never would have been able to introduce myself to your mother—that's true. That's absolutely true." He fixes me in his eyes now. "She had so much energy, Sylvia. And if you saw her. She was beautiful, totally. She was absolutely full of life. I loved her. I did. I was going to marry her.

"It was my sophomore year. Thanksgiving. I brought her home to meet my family. You know what they're like. It was her idea. She insisted. That was the way she was. She was optimistic. She trusted people.

"Now Becky was having trouble at school. I didn't really know much about it at the time. I was away at college. We didn't talk about things in my family."

"Like *we* do that?" I say.

"We're doing it right now," he says. "Right this second, goddamn it." Samantha appears at our table carrying two frosted mugs the size of ski boots and plunks them down. My father doesn't break eye contact with me.

"Here's the big boys for the big boys," she says, performing her line so as not to become involved.

"Thanks," I say, then watch her walk away. Her shoulders are strong, and she moves with confidence and unnatural smoothness, like she's on ice skates. She's good at her job. I'm jealous of how much she knows exactly what she's doing. I feel like I don't know how to sit in my chair, that I could at any second detach and float up. My father waits for me to turn back to him; I do.

"She'd been snatching change and dollar bills from my mother's purse for years," he says, "and she'd graduated to my father's wallet. My father knew, of course. Started hiding his wallet, but every so often she'd figure out where, or he'd forget. Kept making her promise to stop. Clean up."

"Drugs, right?" I say.

"Had to be," he says. "Now, she was a little strange at dinner, Becky. This is the Wednesday before Thanksgiving."

"Strange how?"

"She said she wasn't hungry—and she was always hungry. And she just kept talking. Asking me questions. Asking Sylvia questions. Usually she'd disappear into her room. I thought it was maybe that Becky was growing up. She was seeing herself as more of an adult. That's how much I didn't know. That's how much I couldn't tell something was wrong. And Sylvia seemed to like her. She liked everyone."

"Sure," I say, to show I'm listening.

"What happened that night. There isn't much to it, really. There was a party, one of my old high school friends' houses—his parents were gone. I remember I was so worried. Not about what my friends would think of Sylvia, but what she would think of them. I didn't want to go at all. If it was my choice, we never would have come home in the first place. But Sylvia insisted. Like I said, that was the way she was. So we're at this stupid party. And about midnight my sister shows up. Borrowed my dad's car. Who with I don't know. But she was there. She hugged me. She hugged Sylvia. She was wearing a very strange jacket I'd never seen before. This black leather fringe. It looked expensive. She was happy. She was too happy. But I didn't have any understanding of it then. And maybe I just didn't want to see. I'd had a few at that point myself. I was in the rec room shooting pool, I remember. It was all good. It was all going good. And Sylvia comes over and says she's tired. And she says, 'Becky's gonna run me back to your house. You stay, okay? You have a good time with your friends.' And I think, *fine. Great. Everything's fine.* And that was the last time I ever spoke to her."

"What happened?"

"Becky didn't have a scratch on her. Not a scratch."

I got it.

"Becky was in the car?" I say.

"Becky was driving. She crossed the center line, they said. It was a box truck coming north. Lawn furniture. The car ended up on the other side of the street. I can't think about it."

"She was high?"

"Of course she was," he says. "She was out of control. I should have known." And there's something familiar about his tone, the way he's looking diagonally away from me through the floor into the center of the earth. Resignation. Acceptance of justified punishment. I see he's wrong.

"But Sylvia was the one who chose to get in the car," I say. And my father snaps his eyes to me, in shock that I said anything at all, and he hates me, I see, in the moment. His face is a mask and his eyes are vibrating.

Samantha arrives with the baskets of wings and my father blinks away his face, and I'm surprised by the quick, authentic smile he manages for her.

"Thanks, honey," he says.

"Can I get you anything else?"

"Not right now, thanks," says my father, and she goes. I don't watch her this time. My father gazes upon the insane, beautiful orange of his wings and then, all at once, he lets something go. He looks at me.

"I don't want her in my house," he says.

I consider.

"She's dying," I say.

"She's taking up your room."

"Who cares about that?"

"You know what we threw away for your two years of college? You have

66

any idea what a nurse visit costs? You think they give those fancy hospital beds away? You think we have money for that?" When he says "money," his voice squeaks. He swallows it.

"I'll pay more rent," I find myself saying, though I can't, really.

"Forget I said anything," he says.

"No," I say.

"You let me deal with this—and don't you dare go telling your mother we talked about money."

"I won't."

"I told you the story, okay?" he says. "You know the story. Congratulations. Can we watch golf now? Can I have a moment's rest?"

"Golf," I say. His head is turned away from me and tipped up, to watch whatever's on the big TV over the bar. I turn to see. It's a commercial for razors. "Golf."

WHEN we get home, it's thick pink dusk. There's no message from Jane. My father had insisted on listening to fat-voiced sports radio guys complaining about the defensive coordinator the whole way home. The front yard is empty of shoes. Before we get to the front door, I can hear Sylvie; she's sitting on the couch in the living room with the guitar that used to be mine, singing. I recognize her song. It's much better without the blarping saxophone part. It used to be about, I thought, falling in love with a videogame elf, but she's changed the lyrics and slowed it down: "You can't heal a burn with fire," she sings. Her vocal part is different than it used to be, like she's talking, but to a bird. My father, ahead of me, opens the door and marches across the living room—without taking off his shoes, which he always insists we do—into their bedroom, slamming the door behind him. "*David!*" hisses my mother from Becky's room. My sister keeps singing: "You can't steal what was always yours." She's going to keep singing but then clams up when I stop in the center of the room. She keeps strumming, the way it can barely be raining. I see she has slapped a Black Lives Matter sticker into one of the guitar's curves and, on the body, a bright cat face that

67

has a specific meaning I don't know.

"You don't have to stop when I walk into a room," I say.

"Yes, I do. How was the protest?" she says, agreeing with me not to remark on the fact that our father stomped through the living room and slammed the door like he was twelve.

"Fine," I say, consider. "How did you know I went down to the protest?"

"You know that when you're outside, other people can see you? Or do you think you're invisible?"

"I wish," I say. "Who saw me?"

"You have a nice chat with Dad?"

"Who saw me? Was it Jane?"

"Lots of my friends know who you are, dope."

"You had friends at the protest?"

"Yes. I have friends," she says. "You see the gun guys?"

"No—what?"

"A couple of those open-carry guys decided to visit and freak everyone out. Apparently, there was some kind of incident."

"What is that supposed to mean?"

"You know—pushing and shoving. It's whatever." She keeps strumming.

"Jane's there," I say.

"She can take care of herself," says Sylvie. I consider. She's right. Jane doesn't need me. I'm not relieved. "How was the heart-to-heart with Dad?" she says.

"Those aren't the words I would use," I say.

"What words would you use?"

"You know Dad's first girlfriend was named Sylvia?"

"Yeah. Rebecca killed her," she says, slaps the strings still. She picks out the notes of a chord up.

"He already told you?" I say.

"Rebecca did." She plays the chord back down, slowly, head tilted, listening to herself.

"You don't think it's fucked up?"

"I think everything's fucked up," she says. "Everything." She plays the chord up again, then back down. I sit down on the couch next to her; she keeps playing her chords, up and then, with something newly broken inside of it, back down. "You know it's bad, right? You know it's only months. Weeks."

"What do you think we should do?" I say.

"You tell me," she says. I think about the way my father said "money." I think about the way we can't get hot water for the shower. I think about two weeks ago, when I thought I saw his car in the Popeye's drive-thru when he should have been at work—it probably wasn't him. I almost tell her. I don't.

"I think we should help out," I say. I'm surprised. "All this stuff costs a ton. And we have to figure out how to get Dad to talk to her."

"He'll do what he wants to do."

"I thought you were on Aunt Becky's side," I say.

"I am," she says. "But I'm on Sylvia's side, too."

"She's dead," I say.

"How was the protest?" she says.

"I don't know," I say. "Interesting." I think she's going to say something else, but she doesn't. She's in the state of distracted concentration. The chord goes up, the chord goes down, broken. I know she's still listening, too. "It was good," I say. "There were so many people. It's weird. It's like, it's just a bunch of people getting together all at once. But it's so different than, like, the mall." She considers.

"Being present is the first step," she says.

"The first step to what?" I say. The chord goes broken up and comes back down whole. We sit together, listening to the one chord. I feel like the carpet beneath my feet is very thin ice. I haven't gotten enough sleep for days. I imagine sitting in the passenger seat of a car at night gliding along any of the one billion straight Oklahoma City streets familiar as your own body in your own hallway and then you feel the car drifting left, across the yellow lines, like you are dizzy and the earth is tipping and you close your eyes and the tipping doesn't stop—the road tips, earth tips, gravity fails, you are falling up, into the sky.

I wonder if Jane is awake.

Sylvie has stopped playing the chord and is looking at the fingers of her left hand, considering the shapes they make, the sounds they might make. Then my mother is standing in the hallway.

"She's trying to sleep!" she hisses.

"Sorry," I say.

"I'll be quieter," says Sylvie, looking at her fingers.

I WALK Simon very late, not even that far, but he tires out and there's something in his paw, so I have to pick him up and carry him home again. When I get back, someone has turned off all the lights and the house is silent. I wash Simon's paw in the sink. He is a little heavy, stupid, tired cloud. After, because I don't have a room, I go back outside to leave a message for Jane. I know I can call and her recorded voice will answer right away, because she always sets it to Do Not Disturb.

I hear her voice in the night, a memory. "Hi, Jane," I say to her. "I wanted to say hello. I want to say that I was thinking about you. I hope you are doing okay. I wanted to say hello. Okay."

I hang up.

"Eloquent," I say to the air.

I KNOW exactly what I used to think the goal of being alive was:

A room dark as this night and crowded with strangers who are also parts of yourself. The opposite of the bright plastic separate spaces where my father and mother spent their days staring at numbers and talking on giant black plastic phones. In this room, music: guitars at the volume of good screaming, the drum like your own heartbeat filling your ribcage; music so loud it is the air; music so loud you can't even call it beautiful because there is nowhere outside of it to see it.

It was a wish more than an actual experience.

In the band, when the work was to produce the song, not hear it, that feeling—the paradox of taking it all in and letting it all go at the same time—was always just out of reach. I had to concentrate so hard on my fingers. Behind me, the drums hiccupped. It seemed sensible enough to stop fighting, to give up. I could always put the good headphones on and lie on the bedroom floor and turn the music up loud enough to risk damage, to seek disappearing and almost achieving it.

Something I miss: after playing the songs, after trying to play the songs, slipping down into and through the crowd who create new space, subtly, for you, T-shirt sweated through, as if you were, slightly but perceptibly, radiating heat. Then, after all that noise and rage and struggle and joy, the way it felt to open a door into the world, and breathe, and listen.

I listen to the night city extending around me in every direction, unsilent. There's a voice speaking I can't quite understand.

Saturday

I WAKE UP on the living room carpet. All I see is dim sticky yellow. There is a slice of American cheese over each of my eyes.

"Hi, Connor," I say.

"Hey, dude," says a confident, theatrical pretend-young-man's voice. "I just drove over in my golden Ferrari." I lift the eyelid of one slice. My mother is sitting on the couch above me with a cup of (I know) very hot coffee held close to her mouth. She takes a hummingbird's sip. And then, comically too-deep-serious this time: "I need to go try on Peruvian shoes." It's a pretty good Connor, really.

"Mom!" I say, more impressed than anything else by her character work. At that moment the front door opens. It's Sheila the visiting nurse. She's wearing menthol green today, spotted with bright blue squiggles. From my angle, I can see her face as she sees us and nods.

"Good morning!" she says brightly, unfazed.

"Hi," I say, holding the cheese up above my eyebrow elegantly, like doffing a top hat to her. She continues on her way into the hall to visit her patient. Above me, my mother sips her coffee. When Sheila's gone, I say, "What's with the cheese glasses?"

"Every now and then an idea gets into my head," she says. It's true—one April day she picked me up at middle school in my Batman Halloween costume. "And you looked like you could use some breakfast. Or maybe I've gone around the bend."

"I'm not eating face cheese," I say, peeling first one then the other slice free, blinking.

"What's wrong with food that touched your face?" she says.

I consider. The cheese is shiny. I bite off a corner and look up at the ceiling. I try not to wake up all the way, lying on the familiar living room carpet mid-morning under the Thunder blanket—my socks poking out, my mother in good or at least giddy spirits, for the moment, overseeing my waking. From this perspective and stillness, I can see the barest lingering impression of the lines on the ceiling made by roller paintbrushes who-knows-how-long ago. Like seeing wind in the wind.

But then I check my phone and there is no message or missed call from Jane. I take another bite of cheese. I was hungry, I realize. I did need breakfast. I'm awake.

"You talked to your father?" says my mother.

I swallow.

"He told the story, yeah."

"Well," says my mother. "Now you know." She takes a sip of coffee.

"What I don't get," I say, "is why you want her here so bad."

"Your father does, too," she says. "He just doesn't act like it yet."

"But why do you?"

"Because of love. I prayed about it."

"So because of Jesus."

"I don't much care for your tone," she says, quietly but firmly.

"I know," I say.

"Because people should take care of each other," she says.

"What about how much it costs?"

"What about it?"

"You don't have enough money, right?"

"What's money?" she says. "It's numbers."

"Now you really do sound like Connor."

"What does that mean?"

"Nothing. So what are you and Dad gonna do?" I say.

"This," she says.

A voice from the hall: "Mrs. Bennet?" My mother sets her coffee on the side table and gets up.

"Yes?" she says, on her way. I consider, then toss off the blanket and push myself to my feet and follow, shoving the last of the cheese into my mouth; it's gummy and good.

In the bedroom, Sheila is on her knees on the carpet, poking around underneath Aunt Becky's bed; I see Aunt Becky sitting mostly all the way up, her hands resting on top of the sheet. The TV isn't on; she must have been sitting alone in a silent room. I know the sound of that room without voices: hum of dust, tapping of red wasps against windows gentle as drops of rain.

Sheila glances back at us as we walk in.

"Did you run out of the bed pads?" she says.

"I just moved the box—here. I'll show you," and Sheila gets up and follows my mother out. On her way by, Sheila taps my shoulder once with the cup of her hand, like we know each other, and I guess we do. And then I'm alone with Aunt Becky, who killed my father's first girlfriend. I find I don't know what to do with this new information. It is in the room with us like a person.

"Did you want the window open?" I say to say something.

"Alright," she says. I have the distinct impression she's consciously holding her spine as upright as she can, like at a formal event. I open the window a little. It's better right away—a trickling-through breeze in the crepe myrtles, a car going by, the continuing world. "Ta-da," I say for some reason.

"Thank you," she says.

"How are you doing?" I say.

"Fair," she says.

"That's what I'd say, most days," I say. She smiles at how stupid a thing it is to say.

"Where do you work again?" she says.

"Costco," I say. "I've been there about a year now."

"You like it?"

"It's work."

"You don't like it."

"I like it okay."

"This is the moment when I tell you that you only live once."

"I know."

"Your father told you about me?" she says. I wait. I remember when I was a kid, I could overhear all my parents' arguments without meaning to. Privacy in family homes is an agreed-upon illusion.

There's no need to tell her what she already knows.

"Where were you living before?" I say.

"I was in Texas. Before that, I was in California," she says; she blinks once, then again furiously, then closes her eyes. She opens them. "The best year of my life was in Eugene, Oregon."

"Why was it the best?" I say.

"For the only time in my life, I didn't want to be anywhere else," she says. "And I was in love."

My mother comes in with a stack of bed pads followed by Sheila carrying a box I recognize from my time at Costco as diaper-box size.

"We'll need to ask the young man to step outside for a moment," says Sheila, "so we can fix up the bed."

"I don't know if anyone's called me a young man before," I say.

"What should we call you then?" says Sheila. "The prince?"

"The Prince of American Cheese," I say.

"The prince of being late for work," says my mother.

"I'm right on time," I say and, to Aunt Becky, "Take it easy." I see I've just suggested that a woman who passes all her time in a bed should relax. My mother gives me a look.

"Okay," I say. "I'm gone."

"Don't work too hard," says Aunt Becky.

"We'll see," I say for some reason.

I PULL into work and Jane still hasn't responded. I check and see my paycheck has come through. I can't imagine how much of Aunt Becky's care and medication and apparatus it wouldn't pay for. In the breakroom where I clock in, Boss Jessica is sitting alone at the big round plastic table absolutely housing a purple slice of one of the never-picked-up birthday cakes that mysteriously appear there every so often. She looks up and I realize I am staring at her intense eating, which is unkind, and I look away. She says, "I love cake," with her mouth half full. She isn't embarrassed at all.

"I wish I loved anything as much as you love cake," I say.

"I'm sure you do," she says. "Tell me some things you love. You got that pretty girlfriend, right?"

"Yeah," I can't stop myself from saying. She swallows.

"Your mom and dad. What else?"

"Peanut butter. My sister."

"Peanut butter before your sister?"

"My dog Simon." I think. "Tornados."

"You love tornados."

"Well, when they don't hurt anyone. I really like driving at night far away from the city. I like blue cheese dressing."

"Do you love blue cheese dressing?"

"Sure." I consider. "I love the word 'concussion.'"

"You are something else."

"I love Christmas."

"See?" she says. "You're a big softy."

I THINK about what I love as I make my way through the morning. I love the weight of a roll of nickels best of all the coin rolls. They are also the best coin, not only heaviest but also somehow the roundest. I love the process of changing the receipt roll. I love when an order comes out to an interesting number—$57 even, $77.97, $301.03. I love knowing bananas' number. I love having the good zapper. I love the color of the laser. I love when Boss Jessica snaps in her squat silver key to authorize a void; I love calling out into the void for a void. I love running to the back of the store for an unbroken egg to replace a customer's cracked one. I love the dusty dry, cool empty air above me in the warehouse as the day outside turns hot. I love the new cashier's bright white sneakers.

I tell myself I am practicing mindfulness.

"So what do you love?" I ask Jaden in a lull. He's sweeping the swept-clean aisle.

"What do you mean? Are you gay?"

"What?" I say. He looks at me. "Yes. I'm in love with you."

"Are you fucking with me?"

"I'm fucking with you. The boss and I were talking this morning about things we love. I made a list."

"What, like, your family and stuff?"

"More or less," I say. "It's a mental exercise. Like, what comes to mind when I ask that question? What do you love? What's the first thing off the top of your head?" He pauses his sweep, stops, considers.

"Reverse cowboy," he says solemnly.

"Your first answer is a sex position?"

"Yours isn't?"

"Well," I say.

"I knew it," he says. "Dirty mind."

I GET sent out on carts and take a few moments to observe the clouds. I decide I don't love clouds. What are they, really? Neither sky nor rain.

"I don't love you," I tell the clouds.

I don't love you, I tell myself. *What are you doing? Your aunt is dying. Your family is broke. Your girlfriend is breaking up with you. And what are you doing about any of it?*

I'm working, I tell myself.

I stack the carts and push an unwieldy snake of them toward their home along the side of the store. To push the carts well, you have to feel your way to the balance between the force of the forward vector and the lean against whichever way the line bends. It's hard work, and endless, which is the nature of the cycle of shopping cart use. I don't love pushing the shopping carts exactly, but I love being alive to do it. I love many things about being alive. I love Jane. I do love my family, even my aunt, though love means nothing against her suffering and against what she did. Love doesn't do anything. It doesn't mean anything other than itself.

I knock the tip of the shopping cart snake into the back corner of the bumper of a black SUV the size and gleam of a swimming pool.

"I don't love you," I tell the SUV, and dart up to check. No damage. I am mysteriously disappointed. Even the great stupid shopping cart snake can make no mark in the world.

I GUIDE and rattle the line of carts home and check my phone again. A text from Jane: *Meet me at Taco Bell? When's your break?*

THE Taco Bell is only a Mongolian Grill, a Sherwin-Williams, a PetSmart, and a T-Mobile away from Costco. It's not the first time I have met Jane there. I'd get us a couple drinks that looked like they were scooped out of a tropical aquarium. We'd sit there for a while, and she'd talk about her day. Whatever else I am, I'm a good listener. I listened to her talk about the kid who has the periodic table memorized for some reason, the girl who keeps showing up with bruises on her arms, the third-grade teacher who got divorced and had to start selling her plasma twice a week, what the principal was mad at them about, and her plans: the field trip she wanted to raise money for, the unused space past the locker rooms where there used to be a computer lab, what project she was thinking up for her class and what stuff—markers and notebooks and watercolors, toothpicks and clear glue, and plastic protractors—she'd need to buy to make it happen. I liked listening to her. I thought it was enough.

I see her before I open the door. She's in her red teacher-protest T-shirt and sitting in a booth by the far window, facing away from the door. It's like the bad dream when I say her name, and she turns and doesn't have a face. Her phone is on the table, facedown, and her keys are on top of her phone, and she's covering both with one hand. She's holding herself very upright, like a grown-up. It looks like she's about to leave.

I have the urge to ask someone for help. There's a mother and toddler on the other side of the restaurant—she's on the phone with half a burrito unwrapped in front of her and the toddler is red-crayoning the cover of a magazine. There's no one at the register, though the voice of whoever is running the drive-thru back there is clear—words, beeping silence, words.

I slide into the booth across from her, and she does have a face but it's worse than the dream.

"I just wanted to see you," she says. "In person."

"What have you been thinking about?" I say. She understands what I understand, bites her lip. "I don't want to break up," I can't stop myself from saying.

"It's for the best," she says.

"I don't want to break up."

"We're living in different worlds. You know that."

"We're living in Taco Bell."

"That's what I mean," she says, not angry. "That's exactly what I mean."

"Give me a chance."

"It's not like this is coming out of the blue."

"I'll be different," I say. She looks at me. "I can go back to school."

"You have to want to go back to school."

"I do." She gives me a look.

"I need space," she says.

"Space," I say. She thinks, decides, slides out from the table and up. "What do you want me to say?" I say. I can hear my voice breaking. It is a strange thing to hear. It's a voice of mine I have never heard before.

"I have to think, okay? I'll text you in a few days." Before I can even gather myself to firmly, manfully nod, she turns and goes. It feels undignified, and maybe invasive to watch her go, so I don't. When the door closes behind her, I look at the door handle.

I feel lightheaded.

Taco Bell and I are at fault.

I leave Taco Bell and walk across the parking lot to the Walmart Market to purchase a Honeycrisp apple the size of a baby's head and a block of some kind of pale-yellow cheese that is wrapped in wax paper with Irish-looking letters on the label. I eat the apple and half the cheese in alternating bites, leaning against the trunk of my car in the Taco Bell parking lot, watching traffic. There's no point in looking for patterns when you watch traffic, but it is instructive to try, and fail, and notice at least the pattern in the repetition of your own failures. There is a kind of music in it.

"It's easy," says Connor. We're sitting at a picnic table set up on the sidewalk outside a south-side strip-mall taco shop. Connor's giant michelada is absolutely festooned with shrimp; I gnaw on what is left of my block of cheese. "She wants to date a man with plans, so get some. Start working for me. Get a new car."

"I don't think Jane would be impressed by a new car," I say.

"Fine. I'll make up some reason we have to go to Brussels to meet with someone or other. And then you'll tell her you have to fly to Brussels and she could come, too."

"I don't think making up a reason to fly to Brussels is the right move."

"But if we make up a good one, then it's a real reason."

"You can't just invent the truth."

"Why not? We say we have to fly to Brussels, we fly to Brussels."

"Jane would know there wasn't a real reason."

"Then you make it real!" he says. "It's like your name, right? It's a word. Sounds. But you say it to other people and other people think it's real, right?"

"I don't know if I even believe that."

"Now you're just being stubborn about the natural role of faith in life." He leans over and knocks one knuckle on the surface of the table twice. "We all agree to believe what we say is real is real." He gives me a look like he won the argument. I spread my hand on the surface of the table, fingertips down. Old, hot wrinkled wood is not the opposite of a person.

A city is not the opposite of a person.

I don't come to the south side of the city all that often. The grid is the same; there are lots of the same vague warehouses, fast-food restaurants, and sudden sprawling church complexes. Signs point toward the highway; train tracks cross an intersection at a diagonal. Unlike on the other side of the river, there are no giant office buildings or mansions; there are more mysterious, not-totally abandoned auto body shops; there are more signs in Spanish, and more handmade signs, in much more beautiful colors: a subtly not-bright red and a peculiar warped yellow.

The parking lot for the taco shop, shared with a showroom of used appliances, is mostly empty. A tan minivan floats like an abandoned boat in its dead center. The other table is full of a lawncare crew in their sweated-through long-sleeve T-shirts and workpants; their work-truck is parked right next to their table. I enjoy how neatly the black metal-grate trailer is packed with their tools: the mowers side by side like stabled horses, the weedwhackers and rakes clipped in rows along the sides as in a gunrack, the gas cans and large gray trash can secured to the grate by looped neon yellow bungees. Above the parking lot and traffic, the sky is wholly sunset, watery pinks and oranges. A great windowless Walmart looms in the near distance like the castle of a weak but benevolent king. There is a breeze.

A lifted new white pick-up truck with tinted windows drifts in from the street. Heavy hip-hop booms up from the earth as it aims right for us, headlights blasting; it parks across the lines in such a way as to take up four spaces. The booms boom, and then the ignition is cut. Out of the truck steps a young white guy in a tank top with an enormous gut. He goes in for tacos.

"You ever notice," I say, "how white guys go wherever they want?"

"You're a white guy," says Connor.

"What do you mean?"

"What I said," he says. "You're not just eyeballs, you know." I keep looking. A grandma emerges grumpy from the used appliance showroom, then locks the door behind her. It's hers. She looks up at the sky and crosses herself.

One of the lawncare guys at the other table says something about, I think, no fish, and they all laugh.

When I turn back to Connor, he's somehow already through with his shrimp. "You don't want any food?" he says. He's feverishly scrolling through what looks like something written in a different language on his phone—white letters on a black screen.

"I got my cheese," I say. "What are you doing now?"

"Using the time of you looking around," he says, pressing the screen dead again and looking back up at me. "You can do so much with a free second if you don't let yourself off the hook."

"How's your poem coming?" I say.

"I've got about three hours recorded plus about a hundred pages," he says. "I haven't read it yet."

"Right."

"So what's your decision?"

"About what?"

"About working for me." For the first time, I let the idea all the way into my heart.

I'm standing barefoot in the center of a sea of white-sand carpet, barefoot. Jane sits cross-legged on the carpet, but far away, her face turned to look out a window. There's something burning in the city.

"I have to think about it," I say. His phone rings. He's the only person my age who has a phone that doesn't only vibrate. His ringtone is a siren. He holds up one finger to me and answers.

"Madeline!" he says. I think he's going to stand up and wander out into the lot for privacy, but he doesn't. "You sound incredible. Look in the mirror and tell me what you're looking at." He listens intensely. "Yeah," he says. "Absolutely." He listens intensely. "I'm coming to Dallas. I'm gonna be there in thirty seconds. Yeah. I'm hitting the road. Consider me there." He hangs up. "Madeline has skin like milk," he says.

"Wet?" I say.

"I'm talking about milk in poems," he says, considers. "And her voice. You should hear her talk about metaphysics."

"That is not what I thought you were going to say."

"She's gorgeous, she knows money, she knows ontological argument. What's wrong with that?"

"Nothing, I guess. How are you gonna get to Dallas in thirty seconds?

It's at least a three-hour drive."

"Three hours is the same as thirty seconds. It's just time. We're gonna kill these red beers, then jump in the car and we're there. It's perfect," he says. "These girls—women—she knows—they're beautiful. They're brilliant. They'll change your mindset."

"Jane and I aren't totally broken up."

"That's what you're telling yourself—not what she said."

"So you do believe in truth."

"I believe in how the world functions," he says. I consider. I've got ink on my khakis, and I smell like parking lot.

"I've got work first thing," I say.

"So quit. These girls—it'll be dark, and I'll tell them you're a sculptor. Then you can start with me, day after tomorrow. And you can become a sculptor. Truth."

"I can't."

"When was the last time you were even out of Oklahoma?"

It's a good question. I look up at the sunset, fading into smoggy blueblack at the edges.

"I'm not like you," I say.

"But you could be a more *you-y* you."

"I think less *me-y* me might be the way to go."

"Listen to yourself," he says. "Write your own story. Come to Dallas." I know I shouldn't—I'm on the schedule to open.

"Fine—but you have to get me home to get to work by nine," I say. "I gotta open. I'll think about quitting, okay? But I'm on the schedule tomorrow. I can't just not go to work. Get me back tomorrow by nine and I'll come to Dallas."

"You're giving orders now? Okay. I can roll with that."

THERE is no stacked-up traffic on I-35. A miracle. Connor drives faster than the descending curtain of night but is not pulled over. It's like we are living in the video game where he is the hero. After the surreal imperial casino rises in the nowhere and vanishes, we cross the wide river into Texas and streak into godless dark, stages in a mythic journey I don't understand.

When we start getting into the Dallas Metro, it's like climbing off the beanstalk into the land of the giants. There are too many lanes, the font of the exit signs is too tall, the McDonald's off the highway is too large with too many windows, the streetlights are too bright and too everywhere.

"I just remembered why I don't like Dallas," I say.

"It's like Oklahoma City," says Connor, "except everything is bigger and you can avoid the crummy parts."

"Those are exactly the reasons I don't like it."

We process off the highway into a neighborhood of large, luxury-lawned and tumorously garaged houses resembling Shakespearean theaters stapled onto plantations, with patches of brick and stone, the face of each lit up like the space shuttle preparing for a night launch. Walls, gates, iron fences—the streets black and smooth as water.

"These houses could eat my house," I say.

"The listings for this neighborhood are interesting. If you know how to separate the dark numbers from the day numbers, you can carve into a stream of money easy."

"That sounds poetic," I say.

"Not 'sounds,'" he says. "Is."

"How much poetry is there in the price of a new water heater?" I say.

"A comma," he says, not really paying attention, leaning forward to peer out into the neighborhood's symbols. "I dumped a bunch of Baldwin Barney stock last year. It wasn't doing anything for me."

"That's the brand we have," I say. "It's broken."

"I'm not going to touch appliance stocks in the future. Too much necessity, not enough desire."

"I desire a hot shower."

"You're thinking small."

"Maybe," I say.

We pull up to the gate of a house the size of a megachurch, with what looks like a rounded church spire on one corner and a dark bulging bay window the size of an aquarium's shark tank. Inside the window, quick bursts of blue light. There's a key pad next to the gate; Connor leans out and taps a code into it. I think he's done, but then he keeps going. He doesn't check his phone. Then more. It's a sentence of numbers. The gate unlocks, swings elegantly away. The driveway is a bright gray and subtly textured by whatever specialized tools exist to texture wealthy people's driveways. The driveway ends in a semicircle before the front entry, flanked by paired columns with impressively cheesy sculptural details—grapes and vines. I am surprised to see there are only a handful of cars parked around the circle.

"I thought you said this was going to be a party," I say.

"I know you thought that," he says. He parks and we get out. I have more to ask, but he's already on his way to the door.

"Yo," I say, following, and he opens the door that he knows is open, and we walk into a darkened cavern of an entryway that smells of smoke and lemons. Above, crystals of a chandelier the size of a car flicker in light from somewhere else.

"This can't be her house," I say.

"It's where she grew up," says Connor.

"Her parents aren't home?"

"How would I know?" We're moving down a hallway toward a golden brightness. We emerge into a white and coppery kitchen from a movie set. The floor is tiled in huge slabs of burned and glazed earth. The door for the stainless-steel refrigerator could open into another universe; there are two ovens and seven burners, a silver double-sink, an espresso machine that could also fly an airplane. Light comes from arrangements of tiny bulbs hanging from stiff, spidery black wires in precise arrangements. Below one such arrangement is a breakfast bar and a marble countertop, and seated on the stools there are three young women. They are all beautiful, but I find I am noting this fact from a clinical distance; none of them are Jane. Closest to us is Madeline, whom I have only heard about but recognize right away because she does, indeed, have the confident, analytical air of a philosophy professor: tall, all long neck and anciently braceleted forearms and big dark unblinking eyes. The other two young women are not as tall—one is a redhead with curly hair pinned to the side of her head in a deliberate post-apocalyptic way, and the other is a country-music-video blonde. Oddly, they are all wearing sweatpants and T-shirts, and there are three empty bowls in front of them, as if they were having a sleepover and had just naughtily snuck a second serving of ice cream. I would be more relaxed to meet The Queen.

"I told you he'd come," says Madeline, then gets up to meet Connor halfway across the kitchen and puts her arms around his neck for a kiss; she's a little taller than him, even in socks.

"You're a vision," he says.

"Stop," she says, turns to her friends. "See?"

"You were right," says one. She turns to me then, and I see that Connor's going to introduce me, and I think he's going to say something to challenge me to be more than myself and so pin me in my absurd place: "I want you all to meet Matt—he's a sculptor, mainly super-heated aluminum." "My compadre Matt here needs to get laid." "This is Mattius—he's visiting from Iceland." But he says, "Madeline, meet Matt—he's my oldest friend."

I offer my hand.

"I have ink all over my pants," I say.

"Good for you," she says, takes my hand with easy formality, like she's so used to shaking hands she has a method. She gestures to her companions with her other hand, as if they are on display. "This is Cassie and Anna."

"Hi," says Cassie, the redhead, with a normal-enough quick wave. I nod and wave back.

"Hello," says Anna, with an accent like a Russian spy. It's more like what I expected. I point at her with a finger gun for reasons that are mysterious to me even as I am doing it.

"Yo," I say.

An hour later I am crouched, heart hammering, in near-pitch darkness behind a white couch the texture of a cow, my face pressed into dark, dense

86

carpet that smells of lavender and baby powder. We are playing laser tag in the entire downstairs of the house. This was the source of the flashing blue lights in the window on our arrival. Somehow, I have been placed on a team with two bros who have been, apparently, already playing one-on-one for at least an hour. They both work at First Dallas Energy with Anna and are both named Dylan. One looks like a short movie star, and the other looks like a normal-sized movie star, without a shirt on.

The plan is for me to draw attention with a steady, exploratory frontal assault (short Dylan was very deliberate about the word "assault") while the Dylans split—one sneaking out a bathroom window then around the back yard through the West patio, as it is apparently called, and the other edging around the curtains and under the windows of the great room to outflank whoever is drawn in by my very controlled, strategic gambit.

At first, I am determined to prove to the Dylans I am no liability since they insist they don't need a teammate—that two on five would be totally fair. That feeling lasts until right before the team separates when the short one tells me, "Don't fuck this up, Khakis."

"My name," I said with as much melodramatic, wounded dignity as I could muster, "is T-Shirt."

The room I'm in is, of course, enormous; I can't see the ceiling above me very well, but I can tell it is strange, with dark hollows created by thick wooden beams crossing it at violent, stupid angles. In a far corner, a black piano hovers like a whale.

The couch I'm behind is in what I hypothesize is one of two or several seating areas in the room—part of an arrangement around a substantial glass coffee table which I already whacked into with my shoulder during an especially strategic floor crawl on my knees and elbows. Some glass bowl on top worth more than I make in a year rattled and wobbled and did not fall. I could hear in the hallway beyond shuffling, a giggle. The words "But I can see in the dark" (Connor) and a somehow foreign shushing.

I'm wearing a glowing plastic target attached to the center of my chest and holding in one of my hands a plastic assault rifle that fires strings of blue light. It's illegal, as the Dylans explained emphatically, to use your hands to cover the target, then one winked at me and looked into the floor in a meaningful way, which is why I'm lying on my face.

"Code 3," I say out loud, to no one, part of Dylan's serious plan. I hear more shuffling in the hallway beyond.

Because of my position, I can see a crack in the curtain across the room that looks out behind the house. The light there is oddly shimmering; it must be coming from a swimming pool. I am possessed instantly and wholly with a desire to be in it. Floating alone in a swimming pool at night is like being high, except because of the world.

I see a shadow cross the slice of pool light; I don't know who it is, but I know it's a Dylan. All is going to plan. Except when I turn, I see a green glob the size of a heart hovering toward me; I raise my weapon and fire.

I hear myself say, "Anh!"

"Oh no," says, I think, Cassie, her voice flat. "You got me." She doesn't even have her weapon up.

"Sorry!" I say. I push up to my hands and as I do, the red glowing heart strapped over my heart starts to buzz and flash.

"The darkness has claimed you, T-shirt," says Connor from far away. He's somewhere in the dark room in a pretzel of a pose, his breathing controlled; the expertise gathered from the year he was obsessed with going to the gun range has, at last, been applied.

"How do you know my real name?" I say to Connor.

"One can only hear what is spoken," he says.

From the other side of the house there is a thumping, complex crash.

"Dylan!" says Dylan.

"It wasn't me!" says the other Dylan.

WE'RE all in the library. There are built-in floor-to-ceiling bookshelves packed exactly full of books, leather-bound and cloth-bound, thick, the kind of books a lawyer on TV would have in an office and never refer to. There is an empty desk with a front panel swirled with intricate carvings of corn and snakes, stiff chairs upholstered in maroon-ish leather, secured with brass rivets. On the floor is a cream-and-green, intricate oriental carpet, soaking wet, spotted with shards and panels of thin broken glass and, among the glass, little bits of jerking silvery blue. The window is open; one of the Dylans had knocked over an aquarium by the window when he crawled through it. They stand on the edge of the wreckage, chest to chest, the shorter one pushing forward into the one without a shirt, his chin pointed out and up, digging into the other Dylan's throat.

"Boys," snaps Anna. I see she has found somewhere a black hoodie and has tucked her hair inside it; she's older than I thought and had been taking the game seriously. The short Dylan huffs like a baby dragon, backs off. I see Connor's on the floor then, scooping little fish into his palm. He's kneeling in the shatter of glass—there's already a smear of blood on the heel of his hand.

I tiptoe forward, crouch in the glass, to help. He looks up, wild-eyed. "We need a vessel!" he tells me.

I turn and Cassie, still strapped into her glowing green killed heart, hears and ducks out into the hall. Madeline comes in then, pauses in the doorway to take in the scene.

"There's blood on the carpet!" she says.

"I've got a recipe to deal with that," says Connor.

"You do?" I say.

"You don't?"

I scoop a fluttering fish light as light, transfer it into my other palm, and look back for Cassie and see, over Madeline's shoulder, the face of a man— tall, gray-stubbled, black-and-silver-haired. His eyes are mostly closed. He's naked. There's a scar across his abdomen.

The two Dylans snap to near-military attention; Anna purses her lips and clasps her hands primly in front of her stomach. Connor, crouching, looks up from the floor, wipes the blood of his hand on his opposite wrist. His expression is not of wonder or fear, but a kind of unashamed interest. It's unpleasant.

"Madeline," he says, and she turns and sees, and I expect her to scream, or complain, but she moves directly to the naked man and cradles his bare elbow.

"Come on, Daddy," she says. "Let's get you back to bed."

"Let's get you back to bed," he says with quiet authority, the voice of the man who owns the world, and he allows himself to be led out into the hall and away.

"Is that her father?" I say.

"Who else could it be?" says Anna, angry at me, it seems, as if I'm responsible for the sleepwalking father, the accident, the mess, the end of the game.

Cassie comes back in then with an elegant wine goblet half full of water, its bowl formed from a sheet of glass so thin it could be shattered by a song.

THE pool is as beautiful as I could have ever imagined: the city night above us is a smooth gray blank, the pool is ringed in smooth blue-sky tile—the opposite of the gray blank of the city night sky above—and the light from underneath us hovers us among gently fractured patterns. The water has been heated and is warm as blood.

Connor and Madeline canoodle in the hot tub a stone's throw away; Connor of course had immediately stripped down to expensive shiny underpants; his torso was somehow tanner than the rest of his body, like he'd positioned it specifically in a patch of sun. Anna and the short Dylan sit with their feet in the water in the deep end; Anna is wearing sunglasses. The short Dylan has a shoulder covered in dark red dragons and prominent nipples. The other Dylan sits at a glass table and leans into a glowing laptop.

I'm in the center of the pool, not floating quite as easily as I'd wished: swimming in pants is less than ideal and apparently not as funny to anyone else as it is to me. Cassie is the only other person in the pool. The girls had peeled out of their sweatpants as soon as we came outside—they hadn't been having a high-school sleepover; they'd been blissing out by the pool. Anna and Madeline are wearing complex magazine-ad one-pieces with geometric cutouts; Cassie's swimsuit is swim team plain—blue, fish-scaled, thick-strapped.

She'd jumped in right away, swung directly into doing slow laps, back and forth. Presently she pauses halfway down on the far side of the pool, where she could just stand. I let myself drift my way over, graceful as a boy in a pool in his work khakis. I hover, keeping my face at her level. Her hair is less bright all wet.

"Hey," I say.

"I'm not going to do anything sexual with you," she says.

"I don't know that I asked," I say.

"I had to say it," she says. "I say it whenever I'm over here."

"Really?"

"To be fair, it's true you don't seem like the other guys who hang around Madeline."

"I've never met her before. I'm just tagging along with Connor."

"He's like those guys. But he's also not."

"Oh, he's a big weirdo, however you look at it," I say. "Believe me."

"Madeline says he can see into the future."

"Well, he believes he can. And he's right a lot. How do you know Madeline?"

"Church. And sorority," she says. "She was an art history major too, for a while."

"You're an art...person?"

"I'm a junior associate curator," she says. "I do gallery talks. Assist on provenance research. I'll move to full time when I finish my master's."

"That's cool," I say. "I work at Costco."

"What are you, in executive training or something?"

"I scan the groceries. Sometimes I go out on carts."

"Oh," she says, and I understand what she means and find I'm not hurt.

"What's the deal with her dad?" I say.

"She won't tell me."

"It's happened before?"

"All the time. He went away to some kind of rehab for a while last year, I know that. Though she won't admit it."

"What's the point of pretending it's not happening when it's happening right in front of everyone?"

"You have to see him during the day," she says. "He's like a king." She doesn't sound sad. I don't know what to say.

"I bet he can't swim the entire length of this pool and back underwater," I say.

"No," she says, without judgment. I see she's the sort of person who gets mad if you ask them if they liked a movie. Without another word I duck underwater and find the side and push off pure from the palms of my bare feet. Even in my stained Costco khakis, I am not *not* a dolphin, for as long as I can hold my breath.

Soon I'm in a booth at an IHOP with Connor, Madeline, and Cassie. My khakis are still quite damp. Madeline poured the wine glass full of fish into a half-full black bathtub before we left and insisted she'd "have Marcela deal with it in the morning."

In the otherwise empty dining room, there's a table of drunk college students pretending their silverware is other things. Large men who look like they smell like smoke sit at the counter. I order pancakes. Connor orders coffee and bacon. Madeline orders scrambled egg whites. Cassie orders a grapefruit and a hot fudge sundae.

Madeline is nodding intensely at something Connor is scrolling through on his phone for her.

I ask Cassie about her job.

"We just got through installing a travelling exhibit on large-scale mid-century Color Field paintings."

"The ones where people dump paint on a canvas?" I say, hearing my father's voice in my voice, and wonder why I let him talk.

"A few of them work like that," she says, with the calm and patience of, I realize, a teacher giving a lecture. It's not the voice Jane would use. "But I wouldn't use the word 'dump.' It's more about the colors themselves than evidence of how the painter put the paint on the canvas." I don't know how to respond; I resolve to be only myself.

"I'm not sure what you mean by evidence," I say.

"So if you're looking at some kinds of Abstract Expressionism, you're looking in part at the action of the artist applying paint to a surface— through brushstrokes and other kinds of residue of motion. If you spend some time with a de Kooning or a Pollack, you can articulate in yourself what they were doing with their hands, what direction, what stroke, what physical energy, right?"

"Okay."

"So it's a record of time and intention and body just as much as it is color and line and space. And if you're looking at Color Field, you don't see as much of that evidence of the body and energy of the person who impressed the pigments; you see color and arrangement. If you articulate in yourself motion and intention, it's in the colors themselves, not in the body and motion of an implied creating consciousness. There are some artists that don't even do the painting themselves. It's about the power of a plan in the mind. They write instructions for other people to follow. Or even a computer program."

"What's the point of that? A robot can't write a song."

"Why not?" says Cassie.

"A robot can't write a good song," I say.

"You just have to think more like a robot," says Connor; I glance over and he's still into his phone with Madeline.

"I don't think that's right," I say to Connor.

"It's not about what's right," says Cassie. "Or even what's beautiful. It's about what's possible."

I'm groping for something; I can almost get my fingers on it. Cassie waits.

"I think there's got to be a person somewhere," I say. I am unsatisfied.

"Maybe you'd appreciate this Frankenthaler," she says. "It claims a more conceptually liminal space." She gets out her phone—it's the brand-new giant one, and without a case—the first piece of evidence on her person, other than the art history degree, her self-assurance, and her apparent friendship with Madeline, of the money she must have come from. She's as quick on the phone as Connor. She's holding up to me an image of glowing globs of color. I carefully take the phone to look. Cassie explains, "So she doesn't use a lot of individual brushstrokes, obviously. She's pouring and manipulating the canvas and waiting. Gravity and the materials themselves do a lot of the work. She's in control, but you can't see her hands."

"Okay," I say, looking hard into clouds and shimmers of color in the image on the phone screen that is so sharp and bright it shouldn't be possible. I can almost hear it; the moment isn't unlike a moment of being absorbed in song, in a moment of being alive. I have the urge to put her phone in my pocket to take the image with me. I become aware that Cassie expects more words. I know I need to come up with a good question. "What size is it?" I say.

"A garage door," she says.

"A garage door," I say with delicate seriousness, as if she has answered a subtle question. I realize she and I perhaps have different conceptions of the size of a garage door. I look and imagine. A person-sized vague-fetus in the sky-blue of the pool tile, surrounded by smaller attendant blobs in forest green, echoed in halos of translucent browns, a wavering line like an unlit fuse connecting the elements in an unfinished circle. Ghosts impaled on a chain-link fence, not struggling. Or haunted light bulbs, but in a peaceful way. I imagine a young woman in an empty garage, holding a bucket of pale blue, tipping it almost out but not yet—waiting, wondering. I'm not able to get to the end of looking at it. It becomes again time for me to say something.

"So you look at paintings all day?" I say.

"As much as I can allow for," she says. "I'm responding to emails a lot. Or I'm writing up the catalog, I'm going over copy for the explainers and the mailers and all that. And I'm working on the gallery talks."

"What's that like?"

"To be honest, it's more like giving an oral report in high school than I thought. You talk about the artist's life, you talk about when the painting came into the world, you give a few words about context and technique."

"You don't sound enthused."

"It's part of the work. I do think everyone should spend time with these paintings. I believe a museum should be a place where everyone can experience great works of art," she says. "Not only people like us."

"I haven't been to an art museum since a field trip back in fifth grade," I say before I think, *why did I add that information to the world?*

"Really?" she says. "You should go to New York for a few days." I consider. I don't ask her if the plane ticket is more expensive than a water heater.

"I do like art," I say. I know I'm saying nothing. I have a great desire to say something that encompasses all my impossible and unspoken desires and wishes, like playing the perfect song. "It's not, like, only art," I manage.

"All art is," says Connor, "is a record of the world's energy in the moment of its creation." He and Madeline are listening now.

"Sure," says Cassie.

"Sort of," I say, meaning, no, but I couldn't say why.

"Cassie has an exquisite eye," says Madeline with an aunt's pride, to Connor. "You should see the return on the piece she steered my mother to at the last Miami."

WE glide away from the IHOP after a few hits of what Connor calls "the green wave."

"What do you think?" says Connor.

"Why do you hang out with people like that?"

"Like who?"

"Like the Dylans, for one thing."

"The real Dylan is very intuitive as a market modeler." I don't want to ask which one he means.

"But he's an asshole," I say.

"From a certain perspective," Connor says.

"From many perspectives," I say. "You're not like them." Connor doesn't respond. He's deep in thought.

"Seven!" he says.

"Okay," I say.

Five minutes of traffic lights, then we curve into the highway, and the high hits.

"You and I should work together," says Connor. I'm not so sure. I can't make my mouth work in the moment. Connor takes this as a response. "After all, we get along well. We both have an ability to look at the world with a certain interest, as well as detachment. The difference is I'm able to actualize that perspective. I could teach you." He turns to me. "What?" I suppose my face was doing something.

"I wouldn't call it 'interest and detachment,'" I say.

"How would you describe your attitude toward the world?" he says. I consider.

"It's like trying to lift something without lifting anything."

"Interesting," he says.

CONNOR drives contemplatively on the highway, as if the tires are fingertips tracing part of an infinite scroll. Something in the center of my chest itches. My pants are now more cool than damp. I look out the window and it is as dark as if my eyes are closed, except for the streaks of darker dark rushing through the dark. I see faintly the afterimage of the glowing shapes of the painting between the world and my eyes.

The question arrives like a part of a song: "what do you really love?" The answer, of course, is Jane. One night last summer, I watched her climb up onto the roof of her parents' back porch from the back yard, barefoot, using the windowsill, the angle of the porch support, the gutter. She'd been a little drunk, spotted with drops of the sprinkler. She stood there, above me, the sunset in her hair, triumphant. "Come down," I say.

"From where?" says Connor.

"Nothing," I say.

ALL around us, highway is speaking, even and unending; Connor is recording to the phone in his breast pocket.

He says: "The economies of swimming pools, the correlations with waves of wealth, the model of the behavior of light in a swimming pool at night, the possibilities of highways, the yearly cycle of new car releases and the seasons, the accepted limits of headlights, what the sounds of different road surfaces indicate, lifecycles of highway construction and repair, lifecycles of the adjacent forest, the adjacent fields, climate change predictions in the imagination of adults and of children, inefficiencies in the imagination, what models are approximated by the model of seasonal shifts in weather conditions, what data is meaningful and what data is predictive and what data doesn't follow what it claims to follow. What is the meaning of wind speed and direction and humidity and temperature and time of sunset and atmosphere and moisture. Someone in the world can see the farthest of any human in the dark and doesn't know it, and we have the same eyes. The evolution of bridges and the evolution of birds, the relationship between aesthetics and purpose is always either straining or doubling. Why is a bus never beautiful and a car only beautiful if it's moving quickly, or is a car only beautiful if the culture and the market declare it so? If it isn't possible to predict the future, how is it possible to decide probability? The color of electric light is different from the air, who conceived of the first engine, who can best imagine explosions they don't see?"

WHEN I wake up, there is a roll of money—hundred-dollar bills—nestled into my hand in my lap. It must be a thousand dollars.

Connor is still driving.

"What the fuck?" I say. Connor smiles, takes no offense.

"You were talking in your sleep," he says. "It's nothing."

"I'm awake now," I say. The cash burns. I could never accept money like that, any more than my father could. I snap open the glove compartment to drop the cash in. The glove compartment is empty except for the manual and a small cardboard box. It's labeled bullets. Why does Connor have bullets? I take the box and open it. Vials full of pills.

"What the fuck?" I say again.

"No one thinks a box of bullets doesn't have bullets in it," Connor observes, and opens the bowl of his hand for me to tip him one. I see my Aunt Becky, young. She was high when she crashed. I don't want Connor to die. I set the box of pills back into the glove compartment and close it.

"No, you're driving," I say.

"I'm always locked in," he says. "Since when are you afraid to ride with me?"

"I'm not," I say. I see I was more worried about Connor's life than mine. I don't know what this means.

"Can we have some music?" I say.

I KNOW that I fall asleep, and I'm in my house but underwater. It's like the swimming pool, like daylight is water; I hover. My aunt glides toward me from the hallway, her robes longer and thinner, like the trailing curtains of a jellyfish. She needs something, but I don't know what it is. I somehow know the front door of my house is open.

I OPEN my eyes briefly and see through a million miles of water a silver castle with light in every window. In flashing red letters: Tribute to America Memorial Day Weekend.

We're coming up to the casino.

I dream we are inside the casino and it's brighter than it should be, and I can't read any of the words or numbers. An old woman with purple eyes stares at me. Then we *are* inside the casino. I drink a glass of warm water standing on a thick, green carpet and watch Connor caress a golden machine until it vomits coins.

Then we're back on the highway.

"BRO," says Connor. I snap awake. I'm home. There's fuzz and light in my eyes so I blink, but I can't blink the fuzz and light away—it's dawn, the grass and trees and edge of the sky are coated in a haunted orange aura. My father's car is gone. The front door of my house is wide open. I am certain my aunt is dead.

Sunday

BECAUSE I HAVE nowhere else to go, I go in.

All the lights are on. There is no one in the living room. I hear a rustling, a thumping, a slapped-closed desk drawer, and I imagine the EMTs must still be in the room with my aunt: one leaning into her chest, performing compressions, cracking her ribs with the pressure—as they are supposed to do, I remember uselessly from some TV show, to save the life. Even though she wouldn't want to be saved.

But there wasn't an ambulance out front. And the door to her room is closed. Aunt Becky is asleep. There are no strangers in the house. Everything is the same. Except: across the hall, the door to my sister's room is open and her light is on; her door is never open.

My mother is inside, sitting on my sister's bed, paging through a paper-back book—the sheet and the weird giant scratchy green blanket my sister got at some garage sale have been pulled from the bed and tossed on the floor. The room is otherwise the mess it always is, whenever I catch a sliver of it walking by: clothes on the floor, the bookcase overstuffed, books stacked with their spines facing inward. I'm surprised to see at some point recently my sister has removed all the rock band posters and torn-out magazine pages from the walls, which are now as blank as the walls in my old room and dotted with tiny holes. My guitar perches on its stand in the corner like a sleeping flamingo. On the desk where she keeps her laptop to charge is her laptop, the stickers the same: the rainbow flag one my father made a big deal about once at Panera, the earth, an anthropomorphic cartoon fox from some show or comic. The drawers of the desk are open and shuffled through. My mother hears me and holds up the book to me.

"Look," she says. It's *The Autobiography of Malcolm X.*

"What's going on?" I say.

"Is this for school?"

"Could be."

"This is her handwriting!" my mother says, flipping the pages at me.

"So what?"

"Why haven't I ever seen her reading it? Why's it in the bottom of her drawer?"

"It's a book, Mom."

"Have you seen your sister?"

"Not since yesterday morning."

"She didn't come home last night," she says. My ears open. Something's wrong. I know not to show it.

"I didn't come home either," I say.

"It's not the same," says my mother. "You know that. There's the note."

It's on the desk. She wrote it in neat blue cursive.

It reads: *I'm going to be gone for a few days. I'm okay.*

"That doesn't seem so bad," I say.

"That strikes you as something your sister would say?"

"Not really."

"Did you have any idea?"

"No. She take her phone?"

"And her charger. And maybe a few changes of clothes. Her toothbrush."

"So you know she's going to keep up with her dental hygiene."

"I'm not interested in jokes right now."

"It wasn't a joke. It wasn't only a joke," I say, almost believing myself. "It means she's going to brush her teeth. It means whatever she's doing, she's going to brush her teeth. She's not going to the moon."

"I can't believe we didn't know she was planning something. I knew she was mad at school. I knew she was worried about all her news things. But not like this. Ever since Aunt Becky came, I haven't been paying attention to anything else."

"It's not your fault," I say.

"I'm her mother."

"No one knew," I say. "Dad didn't know." I consider. "Did you ask Aunt Becky?"

"Becky?"

"Yeah," I say. My mother considers, then is up in a snap and across the hall. She opens the closed door with a whip. The light is on, and the TV is off. Aunt Becky is awake, leaning back into her pillow, eyes cracked open; she's been listening to us. She looks for the moment merely hungover.

"Did Sylvie say anything to you?" says my mom.

"I'm sure she's safe," says Aunt Becky.

"What did she say!" says my mother, stepping sharply forward, angry, as if Aunt Becky was a child who had disappeared—which, I saw, she had been, she was, she is. I put my hand on my mother's shoulder to hold her in place.

"I don't know where she is," says Aunt Becky. "She didn't say anything about that. All I know is yesterday she asked me what jail is like."

"Why would she want to know about jail?" says my mother, shrieking a little.

"I'm sure she has her reasons."

"What did you tell her? Why didn't you say anything?"

"She was probably just curious," I say. "I would be." I see that my motivations are probably not a good guide to my sister's.

"She wanted to know," says Aunt Becky, "so I told her. That's it." She shifts—the bones in her shoulders grinding together, tipping her toward one side—and closes her eyes, then huffs air weakly out of her nose. She's in pain; my mother doesn't notice.

"Where's my phone?" she shouts, then plows into me on her way out because I am the door; I open to let her through. She's got her phone in her pocket. I don't tell her.

Then I'm alone with my aunt.

"You need a pill?" I say. She cracks her eyes open.

"And another of those Coors Lights," she says.

On my way to the kitchen, I hear my mother stacking books loudly in my sister's room. There's only one Coors Light left in the back corner of the refrigerator.

At my aunt's bed, I find her with her eyes closed and moving.

"Here you go," I say, offering her the beer.

"Water," she says. I set the beer on the table and pick up the water tumbler, set it down to unscrew the pill bottle and tap out one. "Two," she says. She doesn't open her hand toward me but, slightly, opens her mouth. I place one pill on the tip of her dry tongue, hold for her the straw from the tumbler of warm water. She sucks some in, swallows slowly, like swallowing is a problem she has to think through. We repeat the process, as in a ceremony.

After, I watch her breathe three deliberate breaths.

"Do you really want the beer?" I say. She cracks an eye.

"Open it," she says. I do. That snap and sparkling hiss.

I know enough to set the beer, open, on the table beside her.

"That's better," she says.

"You okay now?"

"No," she says, breathes.

"I'll let you rest."

"It wasn't any worse than the rest of the world."

"What wasn't?"

"Jail," she says. "It was cold and boring, and everyone with a uniform on thought they were king."

"She really didn't say where she was going?"

"No," she says.

"She knows what's she's doing," I say. "She can take care of herself."

"Those aren't the same thing."

"No," I say. She winces, as if I'd turned some screw.

"Do you want to rest?"

"No."

I sit in the chair next to her until she falls asleep.

WHEN I get out of the again-lukewarm shower, my father is standing on the mat by the door, recently returned, shaking his keys in the bowl of his hand in frustrated meditation, like he's about to leave again. He's still wearing one of the shirts he sleeps in—a white V-neck stretched out and see-through in streaky patches. He has more gray hair on his chest than I'd realized. He tells us about his search: last night when she didn't respond to texts about some email from a teacher about a missing assignment, he'd checked her room and found the note and then gone to the movie theater where she sells popcorn and ten-dollar sodas, and the manager said she'd called in sick for her shift that night and, no, she hadn't been acting any differently than she normally did (which wasn't the same as saying she wasn't acting strange, though I didn't say so out loud). Then he drove around for "God knows how long—you wouldn't believe how many teenage punks out in the open puffing up on that electronic pot"—dark parks, empty high-school parking lot, Beverly's Diner, and IHOP. Then he went to the police station to be told that, of course, in most cases these sorts of runaways turn up sooner rather than later, and it hadn't even been a whole day. But they took her description. On the way home, he drove by her friend Julia's house again—the other guitar player in their band who also works at the movie theater and often drives Sylvie to work—and this time knocked on the door to learn that Julia had disappeared as well—and her car, a hand-me-down minivan with a punched-in eye—and had left the same note.

"At least we know she's not on her own," I say.

"You've heard their band," says my father. "You think she's better off with them?"

"They're not that bad," I say.

"I'm going to kill her," says my mother. "When we get her home safe, I'm going to kill her. What is she thinking?" My father digs into his pocket, pulls out a couple folded pieces of paper, and hands them to my mother.

"Look what Julia's father found in her school bag," he says.

I read over her shoulder.

It's a printout of the Wikipedia page for the Great Pacific Garbage Patch, heavily underlined.

"A gyre of marine debris!" says my mother, reading.

"It's just a Wikipedia page," I say.

"He was livid," says my father. "It's all this all the time for them, too. Like it's all our fault."

"It's probably for a report or something," I say.

"Harm to aquatic species," says my mother, paging through. "Harm to humans!"

"Her dad says her room is full of this stuff. Colin Kaepernick kneeling and water protectors and save the gay frogs and all that crap."

"Gay frogs?" I say.

"You know," says my father. "The male frogs that get turned into girls. Because of chemicals." He's furious with me for precisely one breath, then he closes his eyes and presses his fingertips into his forehead.

"But that's just what's happening," I say. "That's just what is."

"What's more important—a frog or a good job? Food on the table?"

"Why does it have to be one or the other?"

"It's all designed to get kids like you all riled up."

"I'm not riled up," I say.

"Your sister's different," he says and, like he's drinking something bitter: "She actually thinks she can save the whole world." I'm not insulted and I'm insulted.

"What's she going to do?" says my mother. "Is this about all that violence at the protests?"

"There's not going to be any violence," I say.

"You got punched in the face!"

"That was my fault."

"You have no idea what's going to happen! You have no idea what your sister is capable of!" I don't know what to say.

"I can't deal with this now," says my father, moving past her through the kitchen. "I'm late."

"Late for what? David!" says my mother. He pauses then, his white back floating in the shadow of the hall like a ghost. He is very old. I have no idea what's going to happen. He turns and comes for my mother, and for half of a breath he's going to strike her, but he never was; he wraps my mother in his arms and presses his cheek into the top of her head, eyes closed against tears, and she wraps her arms around him.

"I don't know what to do," he says.

"I'll find her," I say before I realize what I say.

"How are you going to find her?" says my mother, all at once much calmer.

"I've got some ideas," I say. I don't. "But she's okay. She's not a child."

"She's not a child," says my mother, thoughtfully, meaning, *she's a child*. "She's never been easy. When she was born, she screamed for a week." I don't know what to say.

"What was I like?" I say.

"You were a good baby," she says. "You loved ceiling fans." She considers. "You both made me so happy."

By the time I return from walking Simon, the house has settled into an anxious calm. Even though my sister is gone, there are too many people inside it. My father has closed himself in their bedroom; my mother has installed herself in the chair next to Aunt Becky's bed with a detective novel she's read a thousand times held in one hand and another on her lap with her phone. I brush my teeth, pour into myself a whole glass of water, and stuff one pocket full of a Ziploc of the rest of the jar of honey-roasted peanuts from the jar my father hates anyone else to eat from. I'm too in motion to allow myself to feel tired. I compose a text to my sister: *Mom and Dad are worried. What are you doing? Whatever you tell me I won't tell them. I want to help.* There's no response.

On my way out, I see parked on the curb behind my car is an unfamiliar blue Toyota; I think for a moment someone has driven Sylvie home but then I see—leaning back against the trunk, nodding into her phone, holding a cigarette low in her other hand—Sheila, the nurse. She's wearing mint-green scrubs and over that a normal sweatshirt, gray, zipped up, probably against the cool of wherever she came from. She notices me wandering out to my car and looks up, crouches to rub her cigarette out against the curb, ends her call.

"Are you gonna ask me how it is a nurse can smoke?" she says.

"None of my business," I say. She slips the half-cigarette into the pocket of her sweatshirt without furtiveness. "My friend just tosses them in the street," I say.

"That's not my way. How are things?" she says. I consider. *Stranger, I could say, my parents are afraid my sister is maybe about to bomb the mall because too many trees are being cut down in Brazil. My father won't speak to his dying sister.*

"The same," I say.

"Are you keeping an eye on your folks?"

"I'm doing what I can." It's not exactly true. I imagine for the first time what her days might actually be like: a series of early mornings in unfamiliar houses with death in them. "Your job must be impossible," I say.

"I do what I can," she says. "It's not a lot, sometimes. I know something about what to expect, so I can be a sort of a guide. It's a difficult place to be. In between worlds. If you find yourself in that space, it's good to have someone with you."

"How do you deal with it?" I say. The door and then the door and then the door.

"You can't deal with it," she says. "If you try to deal with it, you'll drive yourself crazy. You live it, and you go on to the next house."

"It sounds draining."

"It is. But it pays okay, and I've got kids." I expect more, but there's no more. "Keep an eye on your folks for me, okay?" she says, heading toward the house, pulling a pair of morning-pink gloves out of her other sweatshirt pocket; she's already at work.

And I'm almost late. But my sister is missing.

Jane, I know, must be awake by now.

I text her, *Hey have you heard from Sylvie. I miss you.*

I erase the second sentence. Send.

Nothing, *dots*, nothing.

No, she says. *Why?*

No big deal, I say. *Just let me know, okay?*

Nothing, *dots*, nothing.

OK.

OPERATION find sister, I tell myself.

"Car," I say out loud. "Display last known location of Sylvie Bennet." It does not, because it is a car.

I drive to the record store. She's not at the record store, of course. It doesn't even open until noon.

I drive to the neighborhood where her friend lives, where my father stopped by earlier, where I dimly remember dropping her off one night months ago for "band practice." All the houses look too much like each other in the light for me to know where I am. A woman in a church dress is angrily misting flowers.

Good work, detective.

ON the drive to work, the church parking lots are full, which always makes me feel lonely without at all wanting to stop and go inside. I wonder again why all our churches are so much wider and flatter than churches in photographs and in the movies. It's like we are all afraid of the sky. Which is fair.

I know my mother is not in her church because she would have already been dressed, pacing around the kitchen, sipping coffee, until it was time to leave. I'd always assumed she was like that because of excessive prudish punctuality; it never occurred to me that it was because something about church made her feel not only connected to God, whatever that means, but also anxious. I know she must be feeling guilty about missing church, even though her reasons for not going are because she's taking care of a dying woman, and because her daughter is missing.

Can I imagine what it is like for her to stand in that pew, shoulder to shoulder with others, and close her eyes to hear and say the same prayer she's heard and said a million times before, and feel not boredom but rightness, comfort?

My mind is a basketball floating on the surface of a pond, spinning.

WHEN I get to work, it's still early enough that the cart returns are empty.

When I enter the main doors, I look up as always into the complex and precise network of beams and exposed pipes and wires, as if the things of this world are in their places and someone knows what they're doing.

Most mornings before opening, in the swept-clean concrete cool, with a slight scent of chemical lemon, a humming imperfect quiet, it seems like it is enough to be alive. But this morning I'm not consoled.

The ghost in my pocket vibrates, but there's no message on my phone.

No one of course cares that I am 45 minutes late. There's nothing to do for the moment other than work.

AFTER half an hour on, my lack of sleep catches me, and each order is a message in a dream: a family direct from church with chipmunk boys in matching blue button-ups and khakis buying the last trampoline. A blonde, beige-purse lady with only muffins and mayonnaise. A small man wearing sunglasses secured by a thick blue cord tugging behind him an exactly covered flat of candy and chewing gum. A man in a firefighter T-shirt with a cart of shrink-wrapped red meat and bottled water. I'm snapped awake again when Boss Jessica flicks off my 4 for me.

"Here you go, kiddo," she says, and from the pocket on her vest hands me a pin the size of a quarter—it's the American flag.

"I don't understand," I say.

"Go on and take the stupid thing," she says. "You don't gotta wear it if you don't want." I see she's got one on her vest, next to her heart. I take it and look at it. I can hear what my sister would say if presented with such an object. She has a song, "Where's your freedom / when you don't have a choice?"

"You seen a flag before?" says Boss Jessica.

"Yeah," I say. "Thanks."

"You gotta go help Jaden with boxes."

"Got it."

"And take it easy with the smoking, alright?" she says. I understand what my face must be. I don't bother to say I wasn't that late; I don't bother to explain that I'd been looking for my sister.

"You're right," I say.

I TAKE the pin with me as I head down the aisle toward the back, swerving along the way once to snag a bite of breakfast sausage in a little paper cup; the lady at the sample station gives me a look I deserve.

I'm through the frozen-food cases and the Aisle of Paper Towels and over the "employees only" chain into the back. There are a couple storage aisles back there and, in the far corner, the loading docks where we aren't allowed to go for liability reasons, apparently. I can see a forklift sleeping fatly like a sphinx and a mustached Costco-man I have never seen before standing near it and becoming more and more interested in whatever is on his clipboard.

In the near corner rests the cardboard compactor. Most days, I love it. It's the size maybe of a pick-up truck standing on end, or the head of a giant robot, all mouth, painted a lovely gleaming green with a grate that swings up and down and a marvelous comic-book-red emergency stop button. Jaden is there, in the middle of a mountain of boxes, leaning up to the compactor, boxcutter in one hand, diving down in a stabbing motion to select another one: frozen blueberries. He's as at home as a penguin on a glacier. There's no reason for him to be in the middle of Box Mountain; he could just as well have worked in from the sides. We are not so different. I see he is wearing an American flag pin identical to mine attached to the thin part of his vest near his collarbone.

"You got a pin, too?" I say. He looks at me like he has never seen me before in his life. I show him my pin. He grabs at his vest like I stole his.

"Oh, yeah," he says.

"What's it for?" I say.

"America."

"No. I mean, why's the boss handing them out? Is it some corporate thing?"

"Nope."

"She wasn't too happy about it," I say.

"Of course not!" he says. "Don't you know the story of today?"

"Oh. Her son got killed in the war. Today's the anniversary? That story?"

"I mean the *story* story."

"I guess not," I say. I slip the pin into my pocket.

THIS is the story:

He's twenty-five. Always was a hard worker, a too-intense kind of good guy. The guy at the party who drinks more than everyone else and insists that no one else is sober enough to drive, but he is, and he does drive, carefully, out to the 7-11 for another 30-pack. At midnight he wants to go to the park and climb trees and has to settle for people hooting at him doing a million pushups. That guy.

His mother didn't want him to enlist in the first place. They weren't a military *rah-rah* type of family. Had one great-uncle who repaired airplanes at a base in Germany, a cousin in the National Guard, but no more military tradition than that. Wasn't pushed that way. But he's a true believer in and of himself. Something in the air in America at that time, something inside him.

Before he goes to Iraq, he gets the whole send-off. Summer barbeque at home, flags and family, all that. It's serious. But people aren't worried exactly. His mother is. But he's not. He doesn't seem like he is. He's the person who handles things.

By the time he gets sent over, the war is calming down. That's how it appears from the news at least. But the news is not the war. The news is a story; the soldier in the war is living a collection of moments. It's like comparing a movie to a hand grenade.

She gets the knock on the door about three months later. The story is an ambush. They were going door to door looking for a guy when they wandered into a bottleneck. The story is he was always volunteering for the lead. He was always the first one through the door. He died trying to shield his friends.

Now the local news goes nuts with this. There's his photo on TV, and there's an article in the newspaper, too. His funeral is something. There's the motorcycle honor guard, police escorts. Overflow at the cemetery. A blasting hot day, a real Oklahoma day, crazy wind. More living people than dead people in the cemetery. They shoot the guns and play the bugle and give her the flag. Folded up perfect. The size of a baby.

Now after the funeral, life keeps going. And it's not that the experience of the ceremony makes her happy, makes her think it's all worth it—the sacrifice of it, his life. But it's a story. It's like the ground, something she can stand on. Something she can tell herself and other people.

A year and a half goes by. Then one day around Christmas, she gets another knock on her door. It's a guy with burn scars up his neck and the side of his face. He wants to tell her about her son. She invites him in, gets him a glass of water. He doesn't drink it. He starts talking. He doesn't ask if she wants to hear it. He just starts talking. It wasn't an ambush. Her son wasn't first in the door. It was a bright day, out on patrol. Giving candy to little kids. Someone thought he saw a gun; there was a firefight out of nowhere. Turns out, there weren't any bad guys. Her son got clipped in the back of the neck by one of his own.

Now the guy telling the story isn't right. She can see that. His eyes are bloodshot and he's tearing up and talking too fast. She tries to get him to stay the night. Calm down. But he doesn't of course. It's hard to blame him. He wants to unburden himself. We all say we want to know the truth, all of it.

The thing about the pins, is she's given them out for years. Back when her son was in basic training, then before he died, then before she heard the whole story, and then after. And every year.

"How'd you know all this?" I ask Jaden.

"I asked her how he died. You didn't?"

"That seems personal."

"How else would I find out other than by asking?"

"I guess."

"I know everything about this place. I once got a blow job back by the tires."

"Okay."

I dig the flag out of my pocket and pin it to my vest, right next to my heart, where Boss Jessica did.

THE story and the box task eat twenty minutes. We have the pile almost cleared when a beeping forklift arrives with more boxes. I think about the Boss's son and say "uh-huh" to more stories from Jaden about what happened during that one ice storm and which cashier dates married guys and the one manager who got fired after the gun he carried jammed into the back of his pants went off and blasted a hole in his own ass. Jaden tells all stories with the same eagerness with which he told the story of Boss Jessica's son—as if they are the same, equal parts of life's rich pageant. The attitude is noble in a way, and also insane. Some things have to be more important.

I can't bring myself to share the story of my sister.

He can't talk while he's pulling the lever that runs the compactor because of the machine sounds, but he watches me with his mouth slightly open, waiting to speak again. I survey the wrapped bales of cardboard boxes that I have helped flatten and press and compact into bricks to be shipped away and then hopefully drowned and softened and pressed and shaped and cut and taped together into more cardboard boxes. I am a wheel inside a wheel.

In the noise, I check my phone. There is a text; I hadn't felt it buzz.

Sylvie says: *I'm going to call tomorrow from a weird number. Answer the phone.*

I write back: *You got it. What's going on?*

She doesn't respond.

There's nothing I can do, I know. There's no thread of connection between us that I can follow to her.

Then I get a genius idea. I open Instagram. It's been a year at least since I've looked at my account. It was never my thing. One positive thing I can say about myself is that I am at least good at wasting time in the real world.

I find her account and scroll back through her posts—a couple posts of some green-haired girl with a guitar from some dark crowded room last weekend. Some song lyrics I don't recognize. Fine. A cartoon boy with an "I Can't Breathe" T-shirt. Fine. A many-hashtagged post of a drawing of her band's octopus. Some shots of the teacher protest at the Capitol stolen from the news, tagged with names I don't recognize. I don't let myself look for Jane in the crowd, and I'm sad that I don't see her. Who I do spy, though, is Doug, the bearded teacher Jane was with. He's standing quite close to the photographer, a bit apart from the crowd, arms crossed, surveying the crowd like they are his army. He's wearing a brand-new Yankees cap. I hate him.

I keep going. A little further in, every other photo is a vivid flash of specific apocalypse: a river's mouth choked with orange and oily mud; a turtle trapped and wrapped in plastic mesh; a graveyard of bone-white coral.

Someone on her feed responds to every photo with a skull and crossbones.

The most recent post, from yesterday, is a quote, in white letters, on a black background: "If you don't put yourself on the line, you aren't any-where." Three likes—one is her friend Julia who is also gone. Another is the person who posts the skull and crossbones—CYR—who commented "It's going down. Monday." A locked account. Something chimes between the vertebrae of my neck. They're planning something. And soon. The other like is from Allison!OKC01, who I dimly remember. They used to be on the same soccer team, used to be better friends. Allison's account: inspirational quotes. Groups of unfamiliar, smiling teenage girls. Lots of shots from Starbucks, from behind the counter: a hand pouring milk, spattered rain on the window, a giant bag of coffee beans. And then there's Sylvie, sitting at the counter, headphones around her neck, notebook in front of her, wholeheartedly giving the ironic peace sign. Then, from ten minutes ago, a Frappuccino from a moody angle captioned, "Just jumped on that late shift grind."

I could DM Allison! maybe—but who knows if that would work, if she'd see it, if she'd accept it. But if I could find the Starbucks she works at. She'd know something about what's going on in Sylvie's head, at least. If I knew where her Starbucks was.

Still, how many Starbucks could there be in the city?

I LOOK up and Jaden's watching me. The compactor halts with a *shwipp* and a comically deep clunk.

"Did you ever hear about JC and the superglue?" he says.

"No," I say. "But I'd like to."

ON my last break, I text Connor: *What do you know about Starbucks?*

Don't touch it, he responds instantly. *Only way to handle public brands is short them on the right day.*

I mean individual stores in OKC. Could you ID one from a photo?

Why would I?

I call him.

There are things whooshing and thumping in the background.

"Are you at the gym?" I say.

"I'm ahead of pace!" he says. He's not even breathing hard. I tell him about Sylvie.

"Why should you care? She's responsible for her own choices."

"I promised my parents."

"What do you care about what you promised your parents?"

"Fine. I'm worried about her," I say. I'm surprised to find out it's true.

"Say no more," says Connor. "I'll engage."

He agrees to pick me up after work for "the grand tour!" He hangs up as he's going up a pretend hill on mile four. "I'm cresting!" he says.

WHEN I go out to Connor's car, it's clouded end-of-afternoon and he's sorting through papers with an uncapped red Sharpie held between his teeth, pointed out. There are scribbles and arrows all over the papers.

"You're late," he manages, swings the marker to the side of his mouth and drops it into the pocket of his black polo. I wouldn't be surprised if he chose to wear the black polo with a pocket for exactly the purpose of holding an uncapped Sharpie.

"A new guy needed help counting out," I say.

"You were hired to work to the hour on the nose, correct? I've seen your schedule. If you don't value your time," he says, "no one else will."

"You've got it all worked out then, Mission Impossible?"

"We have to be systematic about this—how else did you think it would happen?"

"I don't know. Drive around. Figure it out. I was working."

"You've really gotta work on partitioning your mindspace more productively," he says. He passes me half the pages. I see the pages are identical sets, and he's made identical red marks on both sets. He has printed out all the locations of Starbucks across the metro. Certain Starbucks map-pins are circled; certain Starbucks map-pins are crossed out; certain Starbuck map-pins float in the hook of a question mark.

"I got what I could from her social media," says Connor. "She's never completely clear about the location, and there aren't many shots of the store layout as a whole, so it's impossible to say definitively where she is."

"Do you recognize anything?"

"Do I seem like a person who has nothing better to do than go to Starbucks?"

"Sorry I asked," I say.

"Imagine. Sitting down at one of those little tables waiting patiently for my cup of hot squeezed cow foam. Maybe I'll have a sip and catch up on 'the news,'" he says, doing exaggerated finger quotes.

"So what's the idea?"

"From what I could gather, I could at least identify that the Starbucks was the size of a post-recession fast-casual footprint, with doors out into some sort of parking lot or another—so not, for example, a hospital kiosk or in a mall. From what I could see, the colors are greens and blacks, and yellow wood. There's one post of the word 'coffee' painted on cream-white tiles in cursive."

"That could be anywhere."

"So it seems the only sensible path is to visit them all. Process of elimination."

"So your plan is my plan."

"You didn't have a plan," he says. "You had a cloud of general vectors."

"There's one other piece of evidence," I say, surprising myself. "I remember one time we had to pick Sylvie up at this girl's house. She lived out by the lake, not far from where they had soccer practice, so she'd probably get a job close to home instead of, like, out by the Air Force base."

"That's unimaginative," says Connor.

"That's what people are like."

"This is going to be less interesting than I'd hoped."

"It's not a poem," I say. "We're trying to figure out where my sister is."

"Right," says Connor, considers, nods once with ridiculous force. "Right."

We peel out unnecessarily into and through an explosion of freaked squawking grackles.

"So," says Connor, driving well and too fast. "We have to put our minds into the mind of a terrorist."

"What terrorist?"

"Your sister."

"She's no terrorist."

"Who do you think terrorists are?" he says. "Young people who keep their own counsel and think too much and too negatively, so much so that they come to believe that everything is wrong and specific powerful men are in control."

"She's just my sister," I say. "And her songs are just songs."

"Terrorists have brothers and sing songs, dude," he says.

My whole spine buzzes.

"She's probably just planning to march with the teachers," I say.

"Why'd she need to disappear herself then?" he says. "And why are you so desperate to find her?"

"Because my parents are worried."

"Worried about her, or about what she could do?"

"Let's find her first and worry about everything else later."

THE FIRST Starbucks is not far. It's in a newer strip-mall plaza that is fancily roofed to not look like a strip-mall plaza and so looks like ugly houses with name tags. There's a Panera, some kind of store for really expensive eyeglasses, and a tuxedo rental shop. Then there's a Verizon store, then the Starbucks, and on the other side, nothing.

"Do you ever feel bad for a store if it's on the end so it only touches one other store?" I say.

"Stores don't have feelings," says Connor. "They have energy, good or bad."

Inside, it looks like a Starbucks.

"What's the energy?" I say.

"I'm vibing out resemblances," says Connor. "It's difficult. Its vibes are translucent brown." On one wall there are some large framed botanical prints, wallpaper of unreadably large fragments of words. There is a black shiny bookcase packed full of coffee beans, various mugs and presses and travel cups, and European coffee doodads. The tables are matte black circles. A MacBook guy types in a blistering rat-tat-tat. On the opposite side of the store is a rainbow-unicorn-stickered MacBook teenager looking at something bright and swirling. There are also some uncomfortable-looking, leathery, wine-colored chairs. A mother sits in one—baby in the car seat at her feet—flicking through recipe videos. At the register is a neat, large grandma, and behind the coffee machine, a young man with black eyeliner calls forth a hissing of steam.

"It's wrong. There's no stools," I say. "Sylvie was sitting on a stool at a counter."

"On to the next one," says Connor.

DRIVING in Oklahoma City is often disorienting even though the whole metropolitan area is younger than that one famous tortoise and is laid out on an easily comprehensible grid system so everything is right angles and straight lines. You always know where you are, but you could be anywhere. There aren't hills; except for downtown, there aren't tall buildings. There's a Sonic up ahead, a white pick-up in the rearview mirror. There is too much light, or there is too much darkness.

As you move, what you notice aren't individual landmarks but more subtle changes in the nature of the cityscape, as in a change in wakefulness. Drive south from my house, the languages written in the signs in the corner of your eye change, like new voices whispering in the corner of your ear; drive north and the houses bloom and back away, and lawns deepen and expand, and traffic slows in the speed limit, as if against a current. Drive west and you enter the 1950s. Drive east far enough and the people and homes sink and the prairie grasses reassert themselves, always waiting for us, below and around the grid in every direction.

Our current route sets us away from the mall; the big box stores shrink; the emptiness in the parking lots of the strip-mall plazas spreads like gently flooding lakes. It's getting late for a Sunday. There's a stand-alone Chipotle, a Showroom Appliance that's completely empty. We turn left away from the ramp to the highway and there's a McDonald's, a Homeland, a Popeye's, a Wendy's, a Hope Pregnancy Center, a Walmart, and a Starbucks.

We pull in and duck out, head in. It's true it's getting late; we've probably only got another hour. I unpeel my looking: this Starbucks is bigger and emptier than in the one photo. The ceiling is much taller than it has to be, with exposed beams; it should be a home for birds. The atmosphere is pretend-ancient-spaceship-picnic. A long, smooth, black communal table, unoccupied. Its seating is stool-chairs with useless low backs, designed to be uncomfortable so people move along. Along one side overlooking the barista's station this time there's the same little bar area, with tall chairs. But it's not quite right—there's a wall, not a window behind it as in the photo, though it could be a trick of the angle.

A bearded, windbreakered man sits there with a steaming hot cup of coffee, top removed. He's making notes in a reporter's notepad next to an opened Bible. An unsweaty young woman in yoga pants and wireless earbuds paws through the kombucha selections in the cold case.

It's the wrong one.

At the register, refilling the display of biscotti and little packs of nuts is a young woman—Sylvie's age, Allison's age—but she's in a head scarf. Before I can inform Detective Connor we're in the wrong place, he makes his way right for her.

She looks up and smiles.

"How would you like to help reunite a brother with his missing sister?" he says.

"I'm sorry?" she says. Her accent is strongly maybe-British, so much so that her "sorry" is a "sorry" and also another word.

"I like your accent," says Connor. "I have associates in Liverpool and Karachi."

"Can I get you something?" she says.

"Can you get me something?" says Connor. "That's a great question. A relevant question." I can see he's winding up at something. "Let me ask you this," he says. "What is the purpose of a Starbucks?"

"Is Allison working tonight?" I say.

"I don't think there's anyone with that name who works here," she says.

"Right," I say. "Thanks." I put my hand on Connor's shoulder.

"You've been a great help to us," says Connor, and he bows.

On the way back to the car, Connor darts ahead. "I should have planned better for these nonsense Sunday closing hours. We need to prioritize possibilities," he says. "But by what criteria? We can strategize this out."

"Okay," I say. I look up into the bright vast gray lid of the sky and am then visited by a revelation. "Duh."

"What?"

"Sylvie was wearing a black shirt in the photo, right?"

"She was."

"She wasn't up here by Allison's house. She was on her way to work, or she was on her way home. That Starbucks photo has to be at the one closest to the movie theater."

"Why are you only saying this now?"

"It came to me when I was looking at the sky," I say. "I thought you would appreciate that."

"It's true that the sky inspires new structural perspectives," he says.

THE STARBUCKS we aim at, near the movie theater where Sylvie works, is in Bricktown. As we're on the way, I see again how obvious it is that it's the right Starbucks. There are Starbucks closer to her house, and parking downtown is annoying, but these are reasons I wouldn't choose to work there. But maybe you like being busy; maybe being downtown feels like being more alive. Why wouldn't a normal teenage girl choose to work in the busy downtown Starbucks? Missing-person detectives must have to be incredibly disciplined not to always be subconsciously searching for themselves.

Bricktown is the Disneyland of Oklahoma City. It's a bunch of warehouses wearing Christmas-tree lights, the triple-A ballpark, restaurants with large, laminated menus listing several kinds of large cheeseburgers, and the canal, which is the wrong color, even though I have lived here my entire life. The sidewalks are often bafflingly crowded. It is the physical manifestation of the feeling of standing in a long line to play mini golf.

Instead of a metered spot, Connor pulls into the valet parking stand at the new Marriott. "What?" he says to me. I guess I'm giving him a look. "A car is not an object. It's the opportunity to go well where I want to go. I treat that opportunity with respect."

It's Sunday evening, so it's not as crowded as it could be, but there's at least remnants of a crowd milling toward the movie theater, knots of teenagers strategically slouching around the Sonic fountain, tinny canned mariachi horns leaking out over from the sparsely populated outdoor seating area of Fuzzy's Taco Shop. The Starbucks is on the upper level above the canal, above the hipster bowling alley, next to a graphic design thesis project of a sushi restaurant; the sushi restaurant is mildly busy. The Starbucks is tinted glass against what's left of the cloud-blocked sunset; it would fit the photos.

"Let's see what's what first, before we go in hard," says Connor.

"We won't have to go in hard," I say.

"Let's do good cop, bad cop."

"Or we could just ask."

I open the door. It's nearly full. One corner is taken up by a dozen younger teenagers with the tittering false ease of freshmen. A few girls sip on giant-strawed Frappuccinos; one of the boys is actually sitting in a backwards chair with his cap also on backwards, the least punk rock method of breaking society's unspoken rules of respectability. The music is turned up much louder than in the other Starbucks—aggressively luxury-furniture hip-hop. There are a couple people in line: a sparkle-jeans girl on a date with a precisely bearded Mr. Bryce Trucks, a guy on his phone—no one I recognize. But when I scan the register and the barista station, I know immediately we're in the right place, a sensation of suddenly remembering an acquaintance's name. The stools and the bar overlooking the barista station are right, the angle to the window is right and then there, wristing a scoop of packed ground coffee into place, is a dimly recognizable face, a pulled-back blonde ponytail, a neat black visor, a girl my sister's age. Allison. She turns and I see she has her phone—gleaming purple case—shoved barely halfway down into the too-tight back pocket of her black jeans in the way girls like her do that makes me nervous. This is why, I think, she and Sylvie stopped being good friends.

Connor's looking at me with arched eyebrows. I nod.

"Killshot," he says, too loudly, but luckily the steam hisses over him. "Be cool," he says.

"Crystal," I say. "Crystal cool." Connor squints at me. I wander over to the barista station.

Steam hisses.

"Hi—do you remember me?" I say to who I am pretty sure is Allison.

"Garth!" she calls, swirls and slaps down some kind of frothy iced coffee with dark chocolate-colored streaks along the cup's insides. "What do you need?" she says to me.

"You know Sylvie Bennet? From Northwest? I'm her brother."

"Yeah?"

"Has she been by recently?"

"A couple days ago, why?"

"You know where she is right now?"

"Why're you asking me?"

It was time to make the leap.

"Do you know what's going on on Monday?"

"That's tomorrow."

"Why's it important?"

"I have no idea."

"Why'd you like this photo. On her Instagram?" I show her.

"That's a thin polar bear," she says.

"Sorry," I say, find the right one, hand her the phone.

"Oh, I don't know," she says, flicking through. "I like a bunch of stuff she posts. I assumed it was, like, an anniversary or something."

She doesn't know anything.

"Sure," I say. I take the phone back.

"What are you hiding?" says Connor, at my side then, leaning outrageously forward. I grab at him, to pull him back. Allison, though, is somehow not surprised; she gives him a look, wipes down a spout with a white cloth.

"Excuse me?" she says. I guess dealing with a million baked fifteen-year-olds on their way to Avengers 99 every day must deaden your flip-out instinct.

"I apologize for him," I say. I'm about to walk us out. But then I think, *that's exactly what you would do. Where's your sister?* I say, "It's just, he's worried about her."

"He's worried about her?" says Allison, hand on the counter now, leaning, listening.

"She's missing, my sister," I say, lowering my voice, leaning in. "Since yesterday. We're doing everything we can to find her." I raise a knuckle to my eye to rub an itch but then think maybe I should make up that I'm on the verge of tears, and I blink, and then think, *no, that's stupid*, and then, *shouldn't you be on the verge of tears?* And: *no, not yet.* Sylvie knows what's she's doing, wherever she is. She's got a plan. But maybe that's worse. I blink and drop my hand, and Allison is looking at me, like maybe she buys it. "We're all worried about her."

"I honestly don't know where she is," says Allison. "I don't know if she'd tell me anyway. She's changed a lot. I mean, I guess we all change. But she changed a lot."

"What do you mean?"

"At school. She's always hanging around her weird new friends—the band kids. That one guy who got suspended for bringing a Gatorade bottle of vodka on the field trip to the zoo." That's not like her, I think. That's like Becky. "She argues with teachers now."

"About what?"

"Everything. She got so pissed about some stupid Hemingway story."

"Who cares about Hemingway?" I say.

"She does, I guess."

"What was it about?"

"I don't remember."

"That's a dead end," says Connor firmly, like a detective who knows what he's doing—and he does, I guess. "What can you tell us about what she was like the last time you saw her, when you made that post on Instagram?"

She taps the uncollected iced coffee on the counter.

"Garth!" she calls again, loud enough to ring my ears. One of the little dudes from the group of teenagers scrapes a chair back and smirks over to us, reaches across us to snatch the coffee in a motion so performatively confident that if there were any justice in the world would lead to his spilling his chocolate sugar bomb all over his shoes; he doesn't spill.

Allison turns back to her work. Her hands float around the handles and spouts with the unfussy tenderness of a pilot's on her panels of switches and lighted buttons that keep the world in the air.

"It was nice to see her," says Allison, to me, knocking a hunk of pressed coffee grounds into the bin. "It's different when it's just her and outside of school. We talked about old times. Junior prom and stuff like that. She was on her way to work."

"Anything else?" I say. She comes up from a dip to the refrigerator already pouring almond milk into a neat little silver pitcher.

"Well, she was reading up on the teacher protests." Of course she was. "There was some news about something. She knew a lot about it. I mean, I don't care either way. It's nice to be off school, though. I just sort of agreed with her. I didn't want to get into a fight."

"Did she claim any membership in any politically radical organizations?" says Connor.

"What?" I say.

"I don't think so," says Allison.

"Antifa? Democratic Socialists?"

"What's 'Antifa'?"

I step in. "Did it seem like she was planning on going down to the Capitol to participate in the protests?"

"I don't know. Maybe," she says. She ducks down again.

"Do you have any idea where she could be now?"

"Like I said, I don't talk to her much anymore."

"Will you do me a favor and tell her to text me," I say to the space she was in. "If you hear from her? Or if you see her?"

"Sure," she says, up and inching away, back to her work. "Do you think she, like, ran away?"

"I just want to talk to her."

"Got it," she says, reading the cryptic order code stickers stuck on the sides of two cups at once.

"FAILURE is an acceptable outcome," says Connor. "If it's the only possible outcome." He's just finished a phone call that was mostly in English that I didn't understand. We're sitting on a wire table outside of the slow Sonic. Insects float vaguely through the clouds cast by the streetlights. I have a medium Dr Pepper. He has a Dr Pepper the size of an infant.

"But it's not good," I say.

"That's a different kind of judgment."

"Maybe from your perspective."

"Exactly how much are you worried about her?" he says. I consider.

"I don't know. I just have a bad feeling, I guess. I'm worried she's young. I'm worried she'll do something to fuck up her life without thinking it through. And I'm worried about my parents, too. They're right on the edge of exploding." Aunt Becky. The water heater. "Everything would be easier for them if she was home."

"You can't be responsible for someone else's feelings."

"I'm not sure if that's exactly true."

Connor left it, took a long pull from his Dr Pepper. "If I had run away from home when I was her age," he says, "I would have been halfway to LA by now."

"If I was her, I'd be baked off my ass in some basement, like, in Stillwater," I say. And I could feel it. I skip school and drift over to Greg the Lemon's house and we pound a couple Monsters and play *Call of Duty* and he wants to buy weed and his guy says to meet up at a Chick-fil-A in Edmond but he doesn't show, he's waiting on some connection in Stillwater and so we're driving there, blasting ahead of a line of storms out into unsettled yellow-green dusk, into a neighborhood with neat square houses and we pull into one that's the same as all the others and inside there is a big empty room with two guys without shirts playing silent *FIFA* and an outrageously beautiful too-black-haired girl restringing a guitar in such a way as I know for her I am not even there, and it smells like burned food, and sweat, and weed. We follow booming hip-hop laments down a hall toward his guy.

I can feel myself there. It's almost night and I'm sitting on the carpet inside an open screen door with a beer can full of water, convincing myself I'm anticipating each moment of the lightning, and the storm is so beautiful and powerful that to be alive to pay complete attention to it is purely correct. A little later, someone convinces me to drive to the 7-11 through the middle of it. I glide through a stop sign I see but don't believe and then get arrested when I'm asked to recite the alphabet and can't not sing it.

"She's not us, though, right?" I say to Connor. "That's the whole problem with how we're doing this. We're talking about a day and thinking about what we'd do with a day. We're thinking about what we'd do if we had a day away from our usual schedules. You'd go to LA. You'd probably stay up all night, buy a new car, write some new algorithm to tell you, like, how the tides affect real estate. I'd do nothing."

I remember one night when she was in middle school, there was a tornado warning in the middle of the night and when the siren woke us all up to cower together in the bathtub, she wasn't in her room. My parents flipped out. Then the back door slid open and she came in covered in mud, carrying the neighbor's pit bull who they never let inside.

Connor considers.

"I wouldn't buy a car, first of all," he says. "And the tides have a cycle that depends on the time of day, which is probably too confined a cycle."

"Whatever. You get the idea."

"The moon, though. You might have something there. You can think—we could work together, do you see? I could put something together. It would take more than a day."

"What I'm saying is that's what you would do if you thought shit was going wrong. Some people would attack, right? Break windows and whatever. Even blow something up, right? To make a point? You'd go somewhere cool, turn your brain on, see a question and come up with an answer, make something happen. I'd do nothing. But Sylvie would face it. She has some kind of plan."

"Plan to do what?"

"The only thing we know is she's going to call me tomorrow sometime from a different number. So it's gotta be that she's gonna do something to get herself arrested. At the teacher protest. Where all the news is. And then call me after."

Connor considers. "How is she going to manage that?"

"Probably do something nonviolent. You know, like in the civil rights movement. Sit down, go to jail."

"Why didn't she say so, then? At least tell you, so no one would worry?"

I don't have an answer. Connor considers.

"What other actionable human data might be sensitive to predictable cycles of natural phenomena?" he says.

"I don't know, dude," I say.

I TEXT Sylvie: *Don't do anything crazy. You have to go to normal college first to save the world.* No response. *I'll have my phone with me,* I say. No response.

AT HOME I open the front door and my father jerks up from where he was asleep on the couch like I'm a home invader. He is first angry, then disappointed I'm not Sylvie, or even a home invader to be attacked.

Simon assembles his old bones and makes his way to me with some grumbles of weary joy. He is still deeply living his only life. He whaps his tail against the hall table and presses his nose into my knee until I bend to greet him formally.

"Where've you been?" says my father.

"Around," I say.

"You hear from your sister?" I know instantly that saying any part of what I know will only make them worry more. I promise in my head that I will be at the protest, that I will protect her.

"No," I say. "But you know she's not alone. She's with her friends. You guys gotta stop freaking out."

"You tell me if you feel the same way when you have kids."

"I'm never having kids."

"How do you know?" he says. "You're twenty-three. You don't know anything." *That's true*, I manage to keep from saying out loud.

"Where's Mom?"

"You know where she is."

The TV is on mute. The weatherman is alarmed; he stands in the sky.

"You think it's okay that she sleeps in there?" I say.

"She says she has to be with her at night, in case she can't hear her down the hall."

"Why don't you take turns?"

"You know why," he says.

"It doesn't have to be a reason why. You don't have to let it."

"If you knew what it felt like," he says. I don't say anything. "If you only knew. And even then, you try to help her. You try to forgive her. You give her money. You give her whatever she needs. You know you shouldn't. You know it won't help. But it's like there's a gun held up to your head. For years. Years, Matthew. I wouldn't wish it on you. I wouldn't wish it on anyone. I wouldn't wish it on my worst enemy."

"It's different now," I say.

"Between this and your sister—" And that's it. He's staring hard now into the TV. He flicks onto a baseball game.

"How much is a good water heater? To get it installed?" I say. He turns to me.

"You have no idea what you're talking about," he says, not unkind. He turns back to the TV.

"So tell me."

"You don't know the first thing."

"Sylvie is going to be okay," I say. "She's not like me," though I don't know what I mean exactly. He doesn't respond. He looks insanely tired and like he'll never sleep again. Simon has already disassembled himself into a warm puddle at his feet, and all at once I feel weighted down, underwater. There's nowhere in the house for me to stretch out and sleep other than on the couch where my father sits, awake forever, or on the carpet with the dog.

I kick off my shoes and take the recliner. It is a dreamlike fake-mossy green, worn and poky in places with age, and I sink creaking into its bones. I check my phone: nothing. My father turns up the sound to a whisper.

There's a commercial about dogs drinking beer. There's a commercial of friendly grandmas and grandpas in the garden and the kitchen and dancing on a boat that turns out to be a prescription drug for non-small-cell lung cancer. Side effects include nausea and stiff muscles as a gentle silver-haired man offers an apple to a little girl in a sundress. If any chest pain or shortness of breath occurs, discontinue use.

I remember Jane in someone's blue kitchen, a little drunk, eyes closed, hair in her face, swaying to music from another room, a small private smile she didn't try to hide from me.

Then we are hovering above a city at night.

I text Jane: *Hey,* but delete before sending. Then: *Any word from my sister?*

The dots go on, then disappear. They go on, then disappear. It's too late for her to be awake, I see. Why is she awake?

No, she says finally. *What's going on?*

She's fighting with my parents and has been staying at a friend's. No big deal. If you hear from her tell her to text me?

OK. Is everything OK?

Yep. Then: *Sorry to bug you.*

It's OK. Goodnight. I stare at it. There is so much I want to say.

Thanks. Then: *Dolphin emoji.*

WHAT it feels like when someone on a phone call is listening but not saying anything.

THERE is nothing else to do until morning.

I DON'T know much about baseball.

I don't watch it by watching through it for a while. Then I'm really watching it.

The sky is black above the ocean of the grass. A purple, pinstriped player has a wet swoop of dark hair and is carrying an egg in his cheek. He has a significant ass. He leans forward, intent. He has struck out 6 and 7.

The batter stands slightly offstage. He is sharply bearded, with a scribble of a thin gold necklace, swooping red letters across his chest. He takes a practice swing, and another, tight and swift and hard. He enters the magic rectangle with one foot, digs it in, planting the seeds of his toes. He shrugs one arm, tears off and re-sticks the strip of Velcro on the wrist of his glove; he is alone. He steps in with his other foot, turns at last to face the pitcher as he raises the bat above and behind his head, a weapon held inappropriately. They are trying to decide if they are in love.

The crowd is sparse and bright.

There is a pitch, and a wild, graceful, unsuccessful swing.

He steps out of the magic rectangle to perform the ceremony of collecting himself. His life makes sense to him.

I AM sleeping but not asleep. Unfamiliar uncles' voices are communicating urgent and meaningless information; they are telling someone else a story about cities and duels and the flight of the ball. There is music; I feel myself floating in a bright place, the mall. There are words in the air, people passing in all directions beneath entering and emerging from bright stores. I hover in the energy of money and aimless motion and safety.

I open my eyes and open my eyes and the TV channel has been changed. The volume has been turned to murmur. It's a repeat of the news. A shot of the interior of the state Capitol packed full of teachers in their red T-shirts. The marble floors of the Capitol gleam like the names of stores. But the protestors don't move. They stand. A crowd that doesn't move is a threat. They look up. They are listening. No, they are afraid. They scatter outward.

I blink myself awake.

I can barely hear. Someone yelled, "Gun!" No arrests. Investigating. Several state reps have received troubling phone messages, the anchor says blondely. Increased police presence for safety.

The weatherman appears. He is serious as a senator. He stands before a map dominated by concentric ovals in colors increasingly of alien birds in a cartoon.

Storms in the morning, says the map. I read the weatherman's lips perfectly on the word "severe." I know the word "severe" could mean anything. Anything could mean anything.

I see my father is gone. I see I have been covered in a blanket, the Thunder throw. It was being covered that made me dream I was floating.

Monday

I WAKE UP to a hand on my face. My mother hasn't woken me up in any other way than pounding on my door for years and years and years, but now because I sleep where everyone can see I am a part of the common architecture.

It's morning.

"I'm here," I say.

She leaves her hand on my face; her keys are in her other hand. She's wearing the too-bright purple raincoat that has always been a mysterious choice for her.

"Your father left early to look for Sylvie's friend's car on his way to work," she says.

"He's insane," I say.

"He had to do something," she says. "I need to run by HR at my work to drop off some forms so I can get approved for sick leave, and then I have to stop by the pharmacy—you've gotta stay with your Aunt Becky." I can't say I need to get to the protest.

"I've got work later."

"I'll be back well before noon."

"Okay," I say. "Did you walk Simon?" Somewhere in the kitchen, Simon raises his ancient head with a whisper-clinking of the tags on his collar. He hears everything, but the only word that matters to him is his own name.

"Simon's not exactly at the top of my list right now."

"Mom. Everything's going to be fine."

"Stay with your aunt," says my mother, on her way.

I WAIT until the door closes behind my mother to check my phone, wishing for words from Sylvie, but there's nothing. Sylvie has a much clearer map in her head of what a person should do in the world than I do, which would usually be comforting.

I rub water all over my face and drink a glass of my mother's orange juice in the kitchen and then go in to say good morning to Aunt Becky.

Her door is open, but the room is dim. I can feel she's awake; she's sitting up in her bed like a ghost sitting up in her bed, eyes open. I move to turn on the light and she says, "Wait."

"You don't want the light on?" I say.

"It's gotten darker outside in the last few minutes, hasn't it?" she says. I look through the plastic slats of the blinds over what used to be my window and can't tell, but because I'm looking I hear a burst of wind; it gathers and shivers the shadows of leaves. I go to the window and look out through what I poke apart. The dogwood thrashes once, annoyed.

"The wind's picking up, that's for sure," I say. "They said storms today."

"I could tell even with my eyes closed," says Aunt Becky. "I love a good storm. Want to go for a drive?"

"I don't think my mom would go for that."

"Are you an adult?"

"That's a good question."

"Will you at least open the window?"

"Why'd Mom close it?"

"She thought she was helping."

"The rain blows in from that way," I say.

"Even better," she says.

I slide up the window and the house sucks the outside in, then holds a breath. What tells you a storm is coming is how nervous the trees are in windless moments, like children holding themselves still, and a feeling in your skin that everything is outlined in a thin fuzz of electricity.

"Yeah, something's coming," I say. "I should turn on the TV."

"Do it in the other room," she says. "I don't want to listen to those cowards." My phone buzzes and I expect the push notification for a severe thunderstorm watch, or a flash flooding alert, but it's a text—from Jane. Even seeing her name is like being punched in the chest from inside. She says, *Your sister is here.*

At the protest? Can you talk to her?

I can't see her now with they black shirts so many cops here is crazy. Cops treyfg move s ot.

Are you ok? There's no response, not even the little dots to let you know the person is alive.

"Shit," I say.

Dots. *Another bomb threaet caled. In,* says Jane.

Are you ok? I say.

"Bad news?" says Aunt Becky.

"No. I hope not. Sylvie's at the protest and there's stuff happening."

"That girl's got spirit," says Aunt Becky.

Dots, then: *OK.*

"I'm worried she'll do something she'll regret," I say to Aunt Becky.

"Welcome to being alive," she says.

"I have to go down there."

"Of course you do."

"My mom gave me orders," I say. "I'm not supposed to leave the house."

"Neither am I," she says.

WE decide Aunt Becky will accompany me.

SHE is able to force-swallow an extra little white pill. It takes her a few tries; I watch, taste chalk on the back of my tongue. She won't let me help her stand. She stands on the carpet in a zip-up sweatshirt, sweatpants, and socks. She doesn't teeter exactly; she is stiffly though precariously nailed together, like a scarecrow. I wait, watching her carefully, arms ready, trying not to appear that I am watching her carefully with my arms ready. She almost takes a step and decides against it and then declares, like she's giving me an order, "I'm afraid you'll have to carry me."

It's not unnatural. I feel like a useful monkey. She smells like peppermint and baby powder. This close I see most of all her resemblance not only to my father, but to my sister. They have the same resting face of thoughtful annoyance, like they will soon begin performing a difficult and necessary task.

"What are you thinking about?" I ask her, trying to talk normally, like I am not at the moment carrying another adult human.

"Winter," she says. "Snow," and, "I'm trying not to fall."

"But I'm carrying you," I say.

"I understand that," she says, "but I don't believe it."

I settle her in the passenger seat and she says, "It's so cold." It's not cold. I run back inside to get the wheelchair, and a blanket, and to leave a note ("Back soon!") on Aunt Becky's pillow. The wheelchair is also heavier than I assume it is, which is stupid, because it's a metal chair with wheels. It just fits folded in the back seat. When I get back to the car, the first thunder rumbles up from deep beneath the earth.

"It's perfect," says Aunt Becky, as I'm tucking the blanket in around her. I know she doesn't mean the blanket; she means the thunder. I click her seat belt in.

"Safe and sound," I say, like she's a baby. She doesn't dignify my comment with a reply. I start the car and find the weather on the radio.

"Turn it off," says Aunt Becky. "What is it going to tell us that we won't be able to see?" I turn it off. As I back out, she works a hand out from under the blanket, and it's like she's going to pop open the door and lurch out of the car and I stop short; she finds the button to open the window and presses it down, with great effort, as if it resists.

"I can turn on the heat, or whatever," I say.

"Drive the car," she says.

The light has further shifted. It's the kind of light that makes you think you need to rub your eyes to make your vision clear. Smoky without smoke, sourceless yellow-green.

"I can smell it," she says as we take the corner toward downtown. A tree across the street flails, a grief-stricken woman stapled into the earth. There's a man on the sidewalk staring at the sky behind us. Traffic moves evenly in both directions, normal; traffic is more unchangeable than anything in nature.

A splatter and sprinkle of rain on the windshield, whispering against my face from the open window.

"What if it hails?" I say.

"We'll sit under a tree," she says. "You're acting like your father."

"Yeah, well, he takes care of things," I say.

"I wasn't criticizing you," she says. I see I have out of the blue defended him in a way I usually don't.

I add, more softly, "I'd like to take care of things, like he does, but I'm kind of a fuck-up."

"You're definitely a fuck-up," says Aunt Becky.

"Hey."

"Takes one to know one."

"I don't think you're a fuck-up," I say, but I can't make it sound like I believe it.

"It's too late in the day not to face the truth," she says. She's turned slightly to the window, rocking in the warps of the road too much, barely holding her balance, watching Oklahoma City drift past with the too-purposeful interest of a child trying not to fall asleep. Church of the Open Arms. Thanh Auto and Tire. An unoccupied bus-stop bench, an empty garage, Pizza Planet, all eerie and sharpened by the storm air, by the desperation of her looking. What must it feel like to look at the world as you know you are about to leave it?

On the other hand, what must it feel like to look at the world and believe it was in your power to change it? And it was your responsibility?

"What exactly did you tell Sylvie about going to jail?" I say.

"Nothing that affected whatever she's thinking about doing one way or the other," she says. "Don't worry. Whatever happens today, she won't end up like me."

I have no idea what to say to that.

The parking lot at the Walmart Market is the same as it always is; there's a line at the Taco Bell drive-thru exactly not quite too long for me to pull in and wait for one bean burrito with sour cream, if I were in the mood. The bronze dragon at the Chinese Buffet presides benevolently over the parking lot for the buffet and the Rent-a-Center. The ordinary world is where it always is and so far away.

My phone buzzes again. It's Jane.

Its crazy get down here

Five minutes

We're stopped at a red light. I have never before been angry at a red light. It's just the way it is, I usually think. What am I going to do, pray it green?

I wish so hard at it that when it changes, it feels like I made it happen.

In the rearview mirror, in the west, the sky is heavy and black, following us like a slow wave.

The next light is changing from yellow to red as I am through it.

"Maybe you should let me drive," says Aunt Becky.

"You can't even hold your hands up," I say, hear myself. "Sorry."

"Don't say you're sorry when you aren't," she says. We thunk over a gouge in the street and she winces.

"I shouldn't have made you come," I say.

"Nonsense," she says. "I'm enjoying myself."

Soon we peel off south toward the Capitol. Buses line both sides of the street and down the side streets, as they have been. As we approach from the back of the Capitol, it looks like no big deal; there's a steady stream of red-T-shirted and ponchoed teachers making their way away un-urgently enough from the Capitol toward their buses—I assume to find shelter from the rain. Then I recognize in the atmosphere the fluttering of police lights out of sync, and I spot one of the tents the teachers set up leaning, a pole knocked down, and we come around the side of the Capitol to see the majestic blocked-off front steps and the square that is still crowded with protestors, at least a few hundred. They aren't marching now but pressing forward in a loose mass toward the Capitol entrance, and standing in their way is a line of police, blocking passage. In clumps within the crowd are, I see, people dressed all in black.

"We're here," I say.

A boy on a beat-up BMX bicycle sweeps along the sidewalk toward the protest; he's dressed in all black, with a backpack; his face is covered by a black bandana; it isn't a boy—it's a young man, my age. Immediately I know that he's got something terrible in his bag—explosives, a gun. He politely swerves up onto the grass to go around two blonde music teachers, one with eyeglasses on a chain around her neck, who are making their way away from the protest. He has a camera on a strap around his neck.

"I have a bad feeling," I say.

"What's the worst that could happen?" says Aunt Becky.

"I just want Sylvie to be safe."

"I think you want to be safe."

"My parents are worried," I say. "And there's a bomb threat."

"Oh, wow, a bomb threat. Those are always real," she says.

"She's only seventeen."

"So's everyone once," she says, cranes her head back to look up at the sky. "A good rain would wash all this shit away."

"Wash what away? The protest?"

"Everything."

I'm creeping along, scanning for parking spots, phone in my lap texting Jane—*Where are you*—and Sylvie—*I'm here. I'll take you home I'm not mad.*

I spot an ancient minivan pulling out; it has soap words on the windows: "SUPPORT OUR TEACHERS." Those words at least will soon be washed away. I yank the steering wheel to slide into the spot, throwing my hand out to steady Aunt Becky, as if she could have flown out the window. My hand is on her heartbeat; I can feel it. It's insistent but feathery, maybe like all heartbeats.

I park and am quick out of the car and have the folded-up wheelchair on the sidewalk next to Aunt Becky's open door. I try to yank parts of it apart, but nothing happens. It's like a frozen, fossilized silver beetle.

"You know the trick for this thing?" I say.

"Yeah—never need one," she says. I knock it on the sidewalk wheels down—nothing. Again.

A woman who looks like my mother in sparkle jeans coming down the sidewalk is suddenly at my side.

"Here, doll," she says, quickly crouching and grasping bars exactly where I did and easing them apart—easy, for her, as unclenching a fist. She brushes the seat clean with a palm and flops out the footrests. "You gotta be a little bit more gentle than you think," she says.

"I never think," I say. "Thanks."

"Better get inside quick, though—they're saying the storm's cutting through El Reno now."

"We will," I say.

When I look back to Aunt Becky, she's grinning.

"Can't wait until you try to fold it back up again," she says. "Like watching a bird try to use the phone."

WHEN I get Aunt Becky in the wheelchair and wrapped up, I feel like I'm transporting a mummy. I start to quickstep, but the rattle in the chair makes me imagine a wheel peeling off and Aunt Becky tipping into the street. We pass many leaving the Capitol. Some amble, but some move with deliberate speed—talking feverishly into their phones, checking over their shoulders, as if they are being followed. A woman has the weather on her phone's speaker, loud. A man with the red T-shirt stretched across his big belly taut as a drum says to me, "You sure you want to go up there?"

My Aunt Becky answers: "It's okay—I'm dying."

Jane texts, *sw corner*. I know she does a lot with maps in her classes. That's why I bought her an atlas. It was too expensive. It was titled, "The World, Known and Unknown." There was a map of grasses in America, a map of the surface of Mars. Sometimes it was open on her kitchen table.

JUST ahead of the still-emptying parking lot between us and the Capitol are the local news cameras, set up; parked behind them are the news vans, flowering awkward stalks of satellite transmitters. The giant-logo-windbreakered reporters huddle with their cameramen, determine what everyone will see. I know the cameras are on. When we pass them, I will be for the first time in my life on the other side of the TV, where things happen.

I need to find Sylvie, pull her away from what the TV can see.

I don't see her.

The protest feels different. The children who used to be integrated into all parts of the crowd have been shepherded away. No one waves a charming homemade sign.

A few hundred people, dotted with the red T-shirts, are facing, I see, toward the Capitol, as if waiting for gates to open for them, but the gates won't open. It's like the protest has been reduced to an essence, a wordless insistence. They are not all young.

Blocking the way to the entrance I'd used the other day, two lights-whirling police cars. A few dozen police in a loose line in front of the cars—some in useless sunglasses against the storm-light, some behind thick shiny black bicycles that they grip tightly—as if they have to be held back like wild horses. They have the appearance of cyborgs: wires in their shoulders connecting to radios, black straps, complexly velcroed gloves, many-pocketed, many-buttoned shirts crisply tucked into many-pocketed, thick-belted slacks or shorts.

Amid the several hundred protestors, I see a red-T-shirted, gray-haired woman vigorously waving a bullhorn over her head, but she isn't the center; no one is listening to her. No one is listening to anyone. I can't see Sylvie. I have a strange feeling I won't be able to recognize her.

A blast of wind, loud as a voice.

Among the protestors are people wearing the same black of the young man on the BMX. I can't help but see them in the moment as the viruses in the cell, even though I know that one of them must be my sister. I have no idea what's going to happen.

"Can you feel it?" says Aunt Becky.

"This is going to explode."

"The rain. It's about to rain," she says. I look down at her and it's like she's looking up beatifically into my face, but she's looking past me, to sky.

I look up, too. I can see, approaching inevitably as a shadow, the storm. The western half of the sky is turbulent black, flickering. It's very beautiful. Even if it were only a painting, I would be afraid. It suddenly makes complete sense to me why someone might want to paint a giant painting and why someone might want to stand in a quiet room and stare into one. This insight doesn't help me.

"I need to get closer," I say. "But we've gotta get you somewhere safe."

"You big baby," she says. "There's nowhere safer for me than anywhere else. And they haven't even fired the tornado sirens. It's just noise and water."

"Still," I say, already moving.

Then I spot Jane from a distance. She's apart from the confrontation, in a knot of teachers in identical red ponchos—of course they were prepared—on the far corner of the open space, under the symbolic shelter of the shadow of a statue. Near Jane is Doug, the bearded stork. Even in the moment I'm glad to see that they appear to be arguing.

I rattle us right for them.

"Jane!" I say, and Jane breaks her attention from whatever sharp word she's about to say and turns and sees me, and her eyes open wide and I see she's happy or at least relieved to see me and I am bolted through with a complete joy. "Matt!" she says, waves hugely, as if I can see anything except her. She notices Aunt Becky. She is exactly as surprised as if I am offering her a baby.

"Hello!" she says, polite and too breathless to say more, as she would.

"Hello," says Aunt Becky.

"This is my Aunt Becky," I say. "She's staying with us. Aunt Becky, this is"—I can't say my girlfriend—"Jane."

"Charmed," says Aunt Becky, brightly, as if we're sitting down for tea.

"You shouldn't be out here," says Doug to me, like I left too much mess on the lunch table at the cafeteria.

"It's a free country," I say.

"They aren't even part of it," he says to Jane.

"Everyone can be part of it," she says.

"It's not teachers throwing rocks," he says. "It's not teachers calling in bomb threats."

"Is that even real?" I say.

"Yeah, it's real!" he says.

"It's only words," says Jane, but she doesn't sound confident.

"Sylvie's in there somewhere?" I say.

"Somewhere," says Jane.

"I promised my parents I'd keep her safe," I say.

"And it's going to storm," says Doug.

"Sure is," says Aunt Becky.

"We can all see the sky," says Jane with a precise bitterness that is lovely because it isn't directed at me.

There's a sharp beep, loud as a robot seagull, and then, a voice that seems to come from everywhere at once: "THIS IS THE POLICE. YOU ARE REQUIRED TO DISPERSE AND LEAVE THE AREA IMMEDIATELY. THIS IS THE POLICE. YOU ARE REQUIRED TO DISPERSE AND LEAVE THE AREA IMMEDIATELY."

In response, a thwack-tink of a thrown stone ticking off one of the cop's bicycles. They don't react. One leans into another, pointing. They don't know exactly who it came from. One holds out a science-fiction-black-gloved hand with an open palm. I see another off to the side raise to ready what looks like an expensive water gun but must not be. He relaxes, but not all the way.

"See?" says Doug, his voice cracking with exasperation.

"Can you stay with her?" I say to Jane.

"I'm not going to run away," says Aunt Becky.

"Of course," says Jane, and I'm on my way into the chaos and as I am in motion finally not thinking about Jane or my Aunt Becky or the storm. I see I have no idea what I'm doing or what I'm going to say to Sylvie when I find her. I arrow through a handful of red-shirted teachers who are obeying the order, have turned away to leave; they seem more afraid than defeated. The edge of the protesting group has become ragged; it's pulling apart. There is lightning, a few haunted seconds of indistinct arguments and encouragements, and then thunder, and then I am there.

The inner crowd is dense as a rock concert but more turbulent. A PE teacher with eyeglasses held tight to her face with a strap bumps into me trying to get through me and away, and I catch her and she looks up at me, grasps at my forearm, alarmed, then lets go.

"Sorry!" she says.

"No problem," I say though she's gone, then continue. To my immediate right, there's a half-circle of young teachers, Jane's age, circling around a weedy young man trying to start a chant—neck strained into cords, like he's trying to lift himself into the air: "What do we want?" he barks, his voice a toy's voice. The response is earnest but diverse, garbled. Someone hollers what sounds like "Five days!" and another something about "Justice!"

A slip of a black-sweatshirted figure zips beyond the chanting group across my line of vision and disappears into the crowd ahead like a thief running away.

A splatter of rain. I follow.

The loudspeaker message to disperse begins again—much louder than the voice of the chanter, louder than any voice in my head, and then there's a sudden blaring of a robot horn loud enough to hurt and I'm walking into it and, then, a quick whip of a police siren and the crowd that had been drifting apart is now pulling apart. It's not a crowd; it's a scattering of individuals facing in different directions, moving in spastic bursts, knocking into each other. "Fuck!" one barks. A woman barrels into my shoulder and doesn't even pause to look up into my face as she continues past. I have a feeling of red evaporating all around me and I see, uncovered by a receding wave, a much smaller group of black-sweatshirted protestors, twenty or thirty at most. They aren't leaving. They are a lost kindergarten class. One has green hair. They aren't standing in loose groups but have locked arms together in an attempt to mirror the line of police they are facing. The police have faces blank as action figures' faces. They stand, a perfect image of state power: people who aren't people and so can't be moved, can't be appealed to. But I remember the face of the cop who helped my mother change a tire in a carpet warehouse parking lot when I was a child. I sat in the grass with traffic at my back and watched. He knew what he was doing; he whistled through his teeth; he was sweating; he called me "Chief." I can't imagine him among them, though he could be. They are a wall. One chews gum in the rhythm of a machine.

All around me red T-shirts scatter; in front of me the black shirts remain anchored, rocks in heavy seas. I spot Sylvie then. She's wearing a too-big black sweatshirt I recognize right away—one of mine I'd thought was lost. She's not on the line, but apart, on the far side, standing alone like a lighthouse. Her free hand is balled into a fist.

I run for her.

"You've got one more chance to disperse!" says a voice—a human voice, a father's voice.

"Hell no!" says a child.

I'm at Sylvie's shoulder.

"Sylvie," I say. It's like she doesn't hear me. But she turns to me. Letters she's written on her cheeks are smeared unreadable.

"Why are you here?" she says.

"I'm here to get you," I say. "We have to go."

The rain comes. My shirt is instantly soaked through; water runs down my ribs. Light.

"No," she says. Thunder.

"You'll get arrested."

"That's the plan."

"You don't have to wreck your life."

"You're right, Dad. Nonviolent protest is totally going to jeopardize my lifelong dream of running for Senate."

"It's dangerous to even be out here." I glance over at the cop. One sees, and points at me.

"It's worse for other people," says Sylvie.

"This is supposed to be about teachers," I say.

"This is about everything."

"But it's not going to actually change anything."

"How are you so sure?"

"Because I'm alive. Tomorrow's going to be the same as today no matter what we do."

"You said *we*."

"No, I didn't."

"You really believe that nothing's ever going to get better?" she says. "In your real heart?" And I see that she's shivering. She's not cold; she's afraid. She's not standing by herself because she's sure of herself; she can't make herself join the group.

I'm somehow not relieved.

I have the urge to embrace her, which isn't a feeling I often have. But she's giving me a look like I've hurt her, and maybe I have.

"Why are you here, Matt? If it's not important? If nothing matters?"

I put my hand under her elbow, but don't grip; she doesn't shake her arm free.

"Come on," I say. I only have to tug at my wet sweatshirt once to get her to take the first step. For two steps, I don't know where we're going. Then we're walking, together, toward the line of protestors.

When we're there, she locks arms with the thin young man at the end of the line; the edge of a spiked flower tattoo climbs halfway up his neck. He doesn't blink away the rain. He doesn't turn to look at us—he's looking at the line of police.

"I have to go," I say. "I have Aunt Becky."

"You brought Rebecca," says Sylvie thoughtfully, but she's no longer looking at me—she's looking through the rain at the line of police.

The line of protestors clenches their arms together tighter in one collective motion.

I turn away to the rest of the world.

It's still there. The rest of the plaza in front of the Capitol is emptied out. Jane and Aunt Becky aren't where they were by the statue. I'm abandoned; I'm alone. I make my way back through the rain to where they were and glance over my shoulder, and the line of young men and women face the line of police the way trees on a bank face a river.

"YOU ARE REQUIRED TO DISPERSE," says the voice from nowhere.

And responding to the voice of the faceless God, and to an invisible shared impulse, the young men and women as a group drop to the ground, still interlocked. If I hadn't known Sylvie was among them, I wouldn't have been able to see it was her.

The voice from nowhere repeats its order, but it's coming from underwater. Lightning flashes in every individual drop of rain.

I spot Jane and Aunt Becky on the far edge of the parking lot. They're underneath the shelter of two large, impressively sturdy navy umbrellas. As I approach, I see the umbrellas are held firmly by a rotund, red-shirted, pink-faced golf coach and a short-haired, sunglasses-in-the-rain blonde woman in a navy visor who can only be his wife; they are improbably cheerful.

Jane is crouching on the side of the wheelchair, half in the storm; she's holding Aunt Becky's hand.

"Is she okay?" says Jane, when I get close.

"She's staying," I say.

"Of course she is," says Aunt Becky.

"If you scootch in over this way," says the woman in the navy visor, "you'll fit in here just fine."

"Thank you," I say. "I'm used to it now."

"It's slowing down," says Aunt Becky sadly. She's right. Thunder complains, being pulled away. The clouds overhead are already thinning, patches of light gray above here and there, as through threadbare cloth.

I turn back to see the protest and to my surprise the tableau of eternal opposition has been broken; we've returned to the flow of ordinary time. The police have moved forward in pairs; I see they are now crouching around individual protestors. They are holding the protestors' arms behind their backs, wrapping white cords around their wrists, lifting them to their feet. The protestors don't resist. They stand obediently.

The atmosphere of waiting for an explosion is gone. There is no bomb;

there is no gun; there is only what is in front of us. I feel how heavy my clothes are with rain.

The police lift the young man with the spiked flower on his neck and he stands; the police and the protestors are working together, playing their roles, like everything that happens is fated, already written. It is terrible, terrible.

But then the young man with the spiked flower on his neck stands straighter up, stretching, as if suddenly shocked, or inspired, and with a twist of his shoulders and jerk of his elbow the two cops on him stumble apart and he's free.

He faces them, then, as equals.

It's only a moment; he's tackled (the woman with the umbrella gasps), swallowed, pressed into the pavement.

Two other cops lift Sylvie, and she allows herself to be lifted. She allows herself to be held upright, as if she is controlled, defeated. But there is something that I see that I wouldn't have seen, in the set of the points of her shoulders, in the way she is holding her head, slightly, tipped up, into what is left of the storm. There is something new there to see.

"Should you call your parents?" says Jane. I look at Aunt Becky; she's watching the protestors being led away with a twisted mouth, a combination of bitterness and longing I have never seen on a face before.

"Let's get her in the dry first," I say.

THE rain lets up enough for us to be able to say goodbye and thank you to the umbrella bearers before we are even back at the car. Thunder moving away is as loud as thunder approaching, but entirely different.

Jane helps me get Aunt Becky up from the wheelchair and guide her into the car. We are each on one side of her; before I realize it, she is the one leaning in over her to secure the seat belt, get her settled. Jane clicks her in, then closes the door gently and pulls upright. We're standing very close. She smells like rain and sweat.

"You want a ride to your car?" I say.

"Rain's done now," she says.

"Right."

"Why'd you bring your aunt to a protest in a thunderstorm?"

"It's complicated."

"Why didn't you ever talk about her?" she says. She's not angry; she's sad. "Why didn't you tell me you've been taking care of her?"

"I'm not really taking care of her."

"That's not what she says."

"I should probably get her home," I say.

"She thinks I should give you another chance," she says. After a second, I realize I'm holding my breath.

"Yeah?" I say, as nonchalantly as I can.

"Let me know what happens with your sister," she says, not unkind, and turns to go. I almost go after her, but the wheelchair is on the sidewalk.

I open the passenger door and dip my body in to check on Aunt Becky. Her eyes are closed, like she's trying to think away a headache.

"You okay?" I say.

"No," she says, and that's all.

"Let's get you home," I say.

The wheelchair collapses neatly on my first effort, like I know what I'm doing. I stow it.

I feel so much more wet-through when I sit down on the dry car seat.

I get out my phone. It's wet, and it works; the screen of course is full of missed calls and questions.

I CALL my mother and she's pissed. Sheila the nurse called her when she showed up at the house and there was no one home. I say we're on the way. And then to get it over with I tell her that I saw Sylvie get arrested. "You let her get herself arrested?" she says. "How could you do that? Your own sister?"

"She'll be fine," I say. "Calm down."

"Don't tell me to calm down!"

"Okay," I say. "Don't calm down."

DRIVING home I don't turn on the radio. The car's tires whirr and shush along the wet and puddled road. It's not peaceful; Aunt Becky is holding herself tensely still and her eyes are closed, but not as if she's trying to sleep—it's like she's barely able to keep her eyes closed.

I'm a different person.

"I'll help you die," I say. "When it's time. If that's what you want."

A weak half-smile.

"You won't be the one I ask, kid," she says.

WHEN we get to the house, my mother's car is gone—I'm sure already trying to track down wherever they took Sylvie. My father opens the front door as we park, like he's been watching for us out the window. I open the door and get out and hear "the height of irresponsibility" as he comes for me down the walk.

The wet is soaking into my muscles. I have had enough of him.

I walk right past.

"I have to get to work," I say. "Your sister's in the car. Wheelchair's in the back."

"Get your ass back here," he says. I don't turn to argue.

"She's your sister," I say.

I TAKE a lukewarm shower until the lukewarm runs out. When I get out, the TV is on in Aunt Becky's room and the house is otherwise quiet. Simon is asleep where I sleep.

When I go outside, I see that the passenger-side door of my car is open, and the car is empty.

I go to work.

WORK is the same, but every ordinary action feels precarious, like I'm about to drop every gallon of milk, like the conveyer belt will snap haywire and pull my fingers into the machine, like the concrete floor is about to spider with cracks and splinter at the next step, and what is beneath the thin ice of the world?

Still, the 18-packs of paper towels are scanned, the almost-always correct change is counted, the shopping carts are collected.

When I go into the break room with my slice of pizza and Coke for lunch, Boss Jessica and Jaden are playing chess. I have no idea where the board and pieces came from.

I sit down next to them.

"I didn't know you played chess," I say.

"No talking," says Boss Jessica. She is intensely serious, arms crossed, leaning forward with an owl's scowl.

"Yes, ma'am," I say.

"She is so good," says Jaden, who smells like Slim Jims and is down both knights already. "She's beaten everyone today. Vicky and Lucas. Shane from the office."

"How did she play that many games at work?" I say.

"I was off at two," she says.

"And you're still here?" I say.

"What's wrong with here?" she says and sweeps a bishop forward. "Check," she says. "I can see it, if I concentrate. The whole board. It's like the aisles of the store, and I'm inside it, in my mind, and I can sense where things go. It's hard to explain. You ever think about how the brain works? How much it can hold inside?"

"I thought you didn't want any talking," I say.

"I knew you were paying attention," she says.

My mother texts me *she's home* and doesn't respond when I text back.

WHEN I get home, the cars are parked where they should be parked when it is starting to get dark. My mother is on the couch asleep and Simon the dog is dead—until he breathes, and sighs in his sleep, on the carpet by her side. My blanket has been folded by someone, probably my mother, and placed on the recliner. I unfold it and cover my mother with it. She doesn't shift; she's not dreaming; she's too tired.

My sister's door is closed, but there's light from underneath it. I feel an unfamiliar relief. For the moment. But I do know that, whatever is happening with her, it's not over.

I go into Aunt Becky's room and she's awake as a bird. In the chair, my father. The TV isn't on. There's a feeling like they've been sitting together quietly for some time. It's not a feeling of peace, exactly. But some silence between them has been broken. They watch me; it's as if, I see, they've been talking about me, and I have appeared.

"I hope you're proud of yourself," says my father.

"I'm not," I say.

"Oh, leave him alone," says Aunt Becky with healthy sharpness. "He's doing his best." I'm surprised to see that my father doesn't grimace, or snap back. It's like he's heard her voice a billion times, because he has.

He regards me.

"I can't think of the last time I've heard you accused of doing your best," he says.

"That's fair," I say. I consider. "I once built Yoda out of Legos."

"You want that to be on your tombstone?" he says.

"No," I say.

"I don't want a tombstone," says Aunt Becky.

"Me neither," I say.

"Rebecca!" says my father.

"What?" she says.

"I don't know," says my father. "I don't know what to say anymore."

"Your father's told you—about what happened when I was your sister's age?" she says. I look at my father. He's not looking at me.

"He did."

"I think about that girl every day of my life. Do you understand?"

"Yes."

"Because you don't. You have no idea. You don't. And I hope you never do."

"Okay."

"You want to hear a story about your father?" says Aunt Becky. I look at my father. He is looking at his own knee.

"Sure," I say.

"It's not long," she says. I settle against the door frame. "This was a long time ago. Before everything. I was sixteen years old. Now, I was wild. Even then. I know that. I'm not going to say I was anyone else's fault. I'm long past all that. All I will say is that I never tried to be wild. I never sat down and thought, *what could I do to piss everyone off?* I'm not going to say that I couldn't help it. But it was like there were bees in my brain. I could barely sit still. I wanted to do well in school. I wanted everyone to be proud of me. I did. But I couldn't just wave a magic wand and make it happen. But I wanted to. You should know that."

"Okay," I say.

"So. The story," she says. "It's winter."

"January," says my father. He hasn't moved or looked at me.

"January," says Aunt Becky. "Your father, he's a senior. He sometimes goes out. He's not a monk. But mostly he watches TV with Dad until Dad passes out or goes to bed early. But I'm out every night. Even some of the nights when I was grounded, I was out. And most nights it wasn't anything at all. Smoking cigarettes in a parking lot. Beers in a garage with boys. Innocent, more or less. But one Friday night, I don't know why, we end up down in Moore, at someone's cousin's place. People I didn't know. And someone gets the idea that we're all going to drive out to the lake. Someone's got a place out there. The middle of the night, in winter. Sounds like a great idea. We're all in for it, of course. All of us. Without a thought, without thinking.

"My girlfriends pile into their car eager as you can be. And I'm following them in but there's a hand on my elbow and it's this boy. Didn't know him from Adam. Not even all that attractive, if I'm being honest. If I'm being totally honest. I can see his face like he's right here in the room with us. But he says, 'ride with me?' just like that, a question that's not really a question. And I like that. I'm a kid. I'm stupid. I like a voice that knows what it wants. So I agree.

"It's romantic, right? And his car. He's got this blue Buick. And I'm impressed. At first. I think the car is his. That's how stupid I am, right? That some high school kid has his own giant blue Buick. This thing is like a boat.

"And he opens the door for me and I get in, and he's already got the thing warmed up. It's beautiful. It's like in a commercial. Inside it's all velvet. And it flies. We're on the road before anyone else even has their car started. It rides so smooth it's like you don't even feel the highway.

"It's so wonderful I don't think; I did that a lot. I don't mind that he's not saying much. I don't think that it's strange there aren't any other headlights on the road. I figure he knows where he's going. He seems like he knows where he's going. But after half an hour I start to wonder. And he doesn't say much. I try making conversation and he doesn't really answer.

"And I remember the moment. It's not a gradual thing. It hits me all at once. Where am I? Who is this guy?

"I tell him I've got to use a restroom, and he nods in a way that doesn't make me feel better. And there's nothing around. It's Oklahoma. It's winter. It's dark. I'm so scared. I don't know what to do.

"It's another ten minutes before there are lights. And he's not even slowing down. I know it's all over then. It's over. But he leans the car onto the exit. And he parks at the gas station. The place is dead. It's dark inside. There's no one else in the lot.

"'Looks closed,' he says. And then he leans over toward me. He's got his hands on me. Just like that. Of course he does. Of course that's what he had in mind. So I slap the guy. I don't mean I brush him off. I mean I slap him. More like just club him with my hand. Catch him right here, below his ear. I surprise myself. I surprise him, too. He starts swearing and I bolt. I swing open the car door and jump out and he grabs for me. I don't know what would have happened. Maybe nothing. Maybe I was making the whole thing up. But I was so scared.

"I run around the side of the gas station. I don't know what I was thinking. Stupid. And there's a ladies' room back there and by some miracle, the door's open. I go in there and I lock the door behind me.

"He's out there, calling my name, telling me to open the door. I don't know how long I'm in there. I don't say anything. I keep my mouth shut.

"He's says he's going to leave. He says if I don't come out, he's going to leave. I don't believe him.

"I don't hear anything for a while. I mean nothing. I put my ear to the door. It's so cold. I remember I was worried my ear would freeze to the door. And it's so quiet. Just frozen quiet. And then all at once I'm knocked back from the door and there's a tremendous sound, like a car crash. He must have come at that door with everything he had. Everything. But it holds. That lock holds. He kicks it. I see it bend in. And he says my name. Not even loud. Just says it, like a question. And I know I'd never told him my name. I don't say anything. I have to put my own hand in front of my mouth. My heart's about to explode. I don't move for I don't know how long.

"But then I hear his car start. I hear the tires on the gravel. I hear it getting quieter.

"I don't open the door. I don't open the door for I don't know how long. It's so cold. I'm wearing this short jacket and jeans. And that's it.

"When I finally peek out, the place is deserted. It's so dark. But there's a pay phone. Thank God.

"And I go to call my friends. But the receiver's torn out."

She pauses, fixes me in her eyes.

"You have any idea what that would feel like?" she says. I know enough not to answer. "And then I see headlights, on the highway. There's a car coming up the on-ramp. I don't even bother to run. I know it's him. I know he's been waiting me out. That feeling. I know it's going to go bad for me. I always knew that, my whole life.

"But you know who was driving that car?"

"No," I say. Aunt Becky waits.

"It's always been hard for me to really sleep," says my father finally, "when it's late and someone's out."

"It was you?" I say.

"When her friend called our house," he says, "because Rebecca didn't show up at the lake, I was listening in. My father couldn't be bothered to get up out of his chair, of course. But I had a bad feeling. So I went to find her." In high school I always used to get so pissed when I'd come home late, high, and he'd still be up, watching ESPN with the sound off, like he was trying to trap me; it never occurred to me he was honestly worried.

"How'd you know she'd be at that gas station?"

"I didn't," he says. "I had a feeling. And then I saw someone standing there in the parking lot. A shadow. From a long way off."

"Your father—when I see it's him, he's not even mad," says Aunt Becky. "You know what else?"

"What?" I say.

"He's got my old winter coat for me. I never even wore a winter coat in those days. I was too cool. It was giant and white. It was ridiculous. Probably found it in some drawer somewhere."

"It was in the hall closet," says my father.

"Wherever it was. I had no idea, but your father did." She doesn't look at him, but she smiles, a little. But then she shivers.

"That's a good story," I say.

"I think about it a lot," she says. And she closes her eyes and leans back into the pillow. Her head makes no more impression on the pillow than a feather does. At first, I think she's in pain; then I see she's crying. She's too weak to turn her head, or sob. Thin water is pressed out from her eyelids. My father looks, glances at me, then back to his sister. I think he's going to turn away. But then he stands and takes the step to her bedside. He rests a hand on the pillow at the top of her head, holding it, open, half an inch above her scalp. Then he touches her head. Then, unbelievably, he dips his face, delicate as into a lake, to her forehead, and touches her skin with his lips.

I leave.

IN THE living room my mother sits up suddenly, blinking.

"You're home?" she says, as if I wasn't supposed to be home.

"Apparently," I say. She considers, starts to stand like she just realized something she had to do. "Mom," I say.

"What is it?" she says. "What happened?"

"It's fine," I say. "Nothing happened. Everyone's fine. Sylvie's in her room. Dad's taking care of Aunt Becky."

"What about Simon?" she says. He is again a warm puddle, asleep.

"He's fine."

"He hasn't been out."

"I'll take him, okay? You go to sleep."

"I'm so tired," she says, looks off into the house as into a foggy ocean, with dreamy interest, and then she lowers herself back to the couch and tugs the blanket over her shoulder again.

SIMON isn't eager to wake, but once the leash clicks on, he is at least amenable. Outside the dusk is heavy and warm. Simon's little legs click down the driveway, beetle-like. I watch him carefully; he walks in straight lines, conserving energy, only diverting from his path for precise and inscrutable reasons. He becomes wholly absorbed in the scents associated with the back tire of our neighbor's pick-up, a new mushroom, a spot in the grass.

WHEN we get back to the house, Connor's car is in the driveway, too sleek and shining even in the dark. He's in his suit, no tie, leaning back against the side door and exhaling straight-up impressive clouds of vapor from the luxurious rosewood vape pen whose efficiency and elegance he once monologued on for ten minutes. It always looks like he's sucking on a fat kindergarten pencil.

"What's up?" I say. Simon pauses, panting, in an exact spot.

"I've got a question for you," he says.

"You didn't knock on the front door, did you?"

"Naw—I saw you wandering around with your little rat buddy."

"Why didn't you follow us?"

"You were in contemplation. I could tell."

"I guess that's fair."

"Your sister's home, right?"

"How'd you know?"

"She's posted about it."

"Right."

"It was just a photograph of the Capitol with the clouds and a link to a news article, hashtag ThisLandIsYourLand. She's gonna be fine."

"I think so," I say.

"All's well that ends well, right?" he says.

"For now," I say.

"Good. Good. But listen," he says. "I need an answer about the job. It's time. There are disturbances in the jetstream. I'm moving some things around. I need a voice on the phone. I need someone I can trust. I'll pay you whatever, and you know I can. But I have to know now."

"I don't think so," I say right away.

"You didn't even give it a second," says Connor.

"No, but I have—I mean, I've thought about it, in general."

"You have? While contemplating the rat dog in the grass?"

"Yeah," I say.

"What are you going to do then? Just work at Costco for the rest of your life?"

"No."

"What, then? What?"

The answer then appears, clear as the sky above the center of the Costco parking lot in a summer noon.

"Can I borrow some money?" I say.

"You don't want a job, but you want to borrow money?"

"I'll pay you back," I say. "We need a new water heater. And I need money to start classes."

"Classes for what?"

"I'm going to become a nurse."

"You're serious."

"As death," I say, sort of to make a joke, then not as a joke. And I know

Connor is going to be pissed. He's going to grimace, call me small, blind, if not in those words. And I'm ready for it. But he grins, blows up a cloud of fine mist.

"It's your funeral," he says.

summer

THE STORM and the arrests only end the protest for one day. It's true that the next day some of the districts don't return to the Capitol, and the protest is smaller. But it goes on.

Two nights later, I get home from work and my sister—sitting in the living room—is the only one still awake, or at least the only one in a lighted room. We haven't yet spoken; I haven't even seen her out of her room. She's cut her hair shorter—nothing dramatic, but different. I'm obscurely comforted to see she is wearing her green octopus band T-shirt. She is still herself. She's sitting on the recliner watching what appears to be a tween sitcom about kids in bright T-shirts attempting to build a robot in a dental-office-clean fake classroom. She doesn't say anything when I stand behind the couch to watch.

One of the girls attempts to fit an arm into a socket in an obviously silver-spray-painted cardboard robot torso, but the arm immediately falls away, clattering onto a table spread with plastic robot parts. She puts her hands to the sides of her head in a performance of frustration that could be seen from space.

Fake laughter.

"This seems good," I say.

"I can't believe I liked this when I was a kid," she says.

"You're still a kid."

"No, I'm not."

"Why are you watching it then?"

"I'm thinking."

"About what?"

"You really want to know?"

"I really want to know."

"I'm trying to figure out how anyone can care about stuff like this. Even kids. There's something wrong with us."

"It's just a TV show."

"It's not about the TV show itself. It's the Disney channel. It's mass media. It's school. Everything."

"That's a little melodramatic," I say.

"Maybe," she says, keeps watching.

"Why didn't you tell me you were going to the protest?" I say. "Everyone freaked out."

"Because I knew what you'd say."

On TV, a chimpanzee in a lab coat.

"What was it like getting arrested?" I say.

"It wasn't anything. They put us in the van and then took our pictures and then locked us into a cold, creepy room and I had to sit for a while until Mom came. They didn't shove us around or anything. They were real gentle." She sounds disappointed.

"You wanted to get beaten up?"

"No," she says. "I wanted those fuckers to pass the full oil production tax. I wanted better body cameras on the cops. I wanted Medicaid and wind power. For a start."

"I get that all that's important and worth fighting for. I do. But you didn't honestly think you were going to win, did you?"

"Not everything you do is only about what happens," she says.

"That makes no sense," I say.

"You know that summer after you dropped out of college, when you met Jane?"

"Yeah."

"You were in that band, playing random places down around the Plaza and that old tire shop?"

"How do you know about that tire shop?"

"I live in this city, too, you know." It clicks in.

"You went to that show?" I say.

162

"Yeah. And a couple more. Me and the girls."

"Why didn't I ever see you?"

"We stayed in the back. But really, you were never looking for me, so you didn't see me." I file back through what I still held of that summer: faces and bodies blurred with colors and noise. "Sometimes you were really high," she says. "There was this one night after you played you walked right past me, but you were looking at your own fingers. And then there was Jane, and you didn't look at anything else much."

"I guess that makes sense."

"I met lots of people in those places. I learned a lot. A bunch of them got arrested, too."

"Why didn't I talk to them?" I say, but I know the answer.

"This one girl—her hair was crazy green—she said once, 'You have to live like the world is what it should be. You can't let somebody else tell you how it is.' I've never forgotten that."

"Says the girl watching Disney Robot Teens," I say.

On TV, a girl frowns into her phone. She gives it to the chimpanzee.

"That's just for right now," says Sylvie. "I've got a revolution in my soul. You'll see." She watches the show. I settle myself into the corner of the couch to watch too.

THE BILL that eventually passes the legislature is not everything that was asked for. But there is a pay raise. In some back room, a few lines on the spreadsheet are flipped and massaged. Some money for facilities repairs, textbooks. A tax increase on cigarettes and alcohol, of course, to be paid eventually by ordinary people. But also an increase in taxes on gas and oil production—modest, not even to pre-boom levels, but something. Perhaps it is possible to change the world.

THE HOUSE settles into its new life. My mother and father are in and out of the room with my dying aunt, and careful with each other—talking quietly in the kitchen, their heads together. My mother sits me down and tells me my father admitted to her that his hours had been cut. She says not to say anything to him—he's trying to pick up some temp hours from the city government. They work it out so my mother doesn't have to use up all her sick days right away and can even go back to work in the mornings. Which has to happen. I know now about the box in their closet where they keep the credit card bills.

My father's kayak disappears. I catch my mother in the bathroom examining, in the mirror's light, a gold ring.

Soon enough, for every shower there is only one brief fading burst of lukewarm water. I make up a story about overtime and finding and cashing an old check so my father would accept the several hundred dollars I'd borrowed from Connor to put toward a new water heater. We don't replace the water heater.

Some mornings it is only me, alone in the house with Aunt Becky. I do sit with her. All through *The Great British Bake Off*, and again, and then, *Friends*. "Those morons," she says, then lets the next one start. Sometimes we switch over to a nature documentary: the fat grace of arctic seals, a flock of cranes crossing over a gleaming river. These help her sleep. Sometimes she sleeps well, without pain or worry.

Sometimes she struggles, as through a crowded room.

WHEN I stop to think about it, I see how strange it is how quickly and completely the house—our family, I—adapt to living with a stranger, with death. But sickness and death are less in the front of my mind than I would have predicted. Not that I don't take it seriously. I do. She becomes part of our lives and our house in her dying. Her room isn't separate.

Sylvie sometimes goes in to sing her songs. When she wants to sing the words, she closes the door so the rest of us can't hear.

I don't believe my father and his sister have any more of a heart-to-heart than what happened on the day Sylvie was arrested. When he's in her room, I don't hear much conversation, even small talk. When I poke my head in, he is often reading the paper, or she's asleep, or he's asleep. But he's there. I can't imagine how a few days' conversation could mean anything up against all those years. What is happening between them is something different from a reconciliation. There is something begrudging and resistant about it, on her part as well as his. But there they are, in the same room.

Aunt Becky is getting worse. That much is clear. It isn't a straight line. Sometimes I come home from work and wander in to check on her and she's sitting up, alert as a schoolteacher, as if she'd been waiting for me. She asks about Jane in such a knowing, fairy-tale-witch way that I don't at all feel bad about not telling her much. It seems to satisfy her that Jane exists. I tell her about work. I never know what else to say. She tells me about her "good years" in California and Oregon. She tells me the story about the day she chained herself together with several others in a human ring around an ancient redwood in an effort to save it from a timber company. She tells me how she didn't really care about protecting that tree until she was actually doing it. How the trunk of the tree was still warm into the evening, alive, how she swore she could feel the life in it when she pressed her whole body against it, like blood in her own veins. She tells me what it felt like when the police van arrived, the men with bolt cutters, what it felt like being pulled away from her friends and the tree and the forest.

The smell of the ocean, even from far away.

Sometimes she closes her eyes as against a terrible light and is not able to answer when I ask if she needs more pain medicine, which means she does. Sometimes she is asleep and breathing through an inch of water. Sometimes she coughs and is not able to cough and my mother stands next to her and smooths her hair.

Sheila the nurse comes most days, usually in the morning when I'm getting ready for the day. She walks through the front door and says good morning as if she's welcoming me home. I help how I can—which isn't much—bring in the clean linens from the dryer. I watch her check on Aunt Becky. There's nothing remarkable about what she does; there is no medical miracle possible, no solvable problem. She checks Aunt Becky's blood pressure, listens to her heart and lungs with an unremarkable stethoscope, holds her thin wrist in her fingers, asks questions about her breathing, about her pain. There is a gentle but unsentimental efficiency in the rhythms of her presence and her actions.

On her way out, she asks if I am looking after everyone. I say I am, more or less not lying. Once, I get up the courage to ask: in her experience, how long? She says, it could be a day, it could be a week, it could be a month. That sounds like forever, I say. It is and it isn't, she says. On her key-ring are a plastic seagull and a photograph of a baby.

CONNOR becomes obsessed with bicycles. It happens in one second. We are driving on our way to purchase audio cords for some complex connection between speakers I don't understand, and a white van pulling stupidly out of a strip mall makes Connor jerk his car to a halt. He's pleased as always with his brakes and tires. In that strip mall is a bike shop. We pull in and Connor buys three and convinces the wiry hippie working there to drop them off later in his van for fifty bucks.

Connor's apartment is soon an explosion of tools and bike parts, more like an operating room than like an engineer's workroom in the organic enthusiasm of the mess. One day there are several new very bright lights on stands with snake-like, mechanical adjustable necks.

He enjoys talking me through his decisions about specific parts of the bicycles. He isn't at all angry with me for my refusal of his job offer. His computers whirr and blink and breathe.

At one point I ask him if he's going to hire the person he'd said he needed to help him.

"It turns out I don't have to move into that mode," he says. "I can let things develop."

"So you didn't really need me?"

"I'm in control of the mode. I can sit back and let the index funds go. The uncle money cycles in every couple months, and there's nothing wrong with letting it earn quiet right now."

"Uncle money?"

"Yeah, the mineral rights from the family land in the basin; you know about that."

"I do now," I say.

"How couldn't you know?" he says. "All energy has an origin. Where did you imagine all this is coming from?"

"I don't know. I thought you were making it all happen."

"You ride the river; you don't invent it."

"Got it," I say.

WE GO out on lots of bike rides around the city. Something I forgot about riding a bike is that riding a bike is awesome. Nowhere else in life can you be as fast and smooth and quiet and only yourself. And, because of Connor's investments in money—and also time, and brain, and heart—the clicks between gears are both buttery and precise; the pavement slides by under us like water over water.

Traffic is traffic, always, during the day and early evenings. But early in the morning, the city is the prairie, the shadows are alive, and the light is clear and red, and the heat of the day can almost be outrun.

One such early summer morning with our backs to the river and downtown before us, even its tallest buildings against the size of the sky modest and delicate as glass flowers, I ask Connor if he has achieved his goal of becoming a poet.

"How can anyone truly achieve becoming?" he says.

JANE'S school is toward downtown from my house, right off a busy intersection with a Walgreens and another Taco Bell on opposite corners. The playground is separated from steady traffic by only a sidewalk and a sturdy black fence; the windows are chicken-wired against shattering and always shaded against the usual Oklahoma City too-much sunlight. The school is a brick rectangle not unlike a small prison, except for, perhaps, the front doors, which are a defiant bright blue. Her school runs several academic summer programs for at-risk youth, partially funded through outrageously complicated grants she alone has the patience to process. At 3:30 p.m. exactly, children in their drab navy and khaki emerge cheerful and wild-armed and weird-teethed and cartoon-backpacked, like children.

I know this only because Jane has several times texted me to see if I am free to meet her after work and I always am, even if I have to shift around my break with Jaden to carve out a good forty-five. I wait for her, leaning on the trunk of my car in the summer heat I know as well as my own body.

When she appears, I tell her we don't have to go to Taco Bell. She says I'd rather go there than pay five bucks for a cup of coffee in a room that smells like incense. I love you, I say, to be funny, meaning it.

We order and sit. I pay. I get the most enormous size Baja Blasts to be funny, meaning it.

I ask her about her work. She asks about my Aunt Becky. She asks about my sister. She asks about my plans. I tell her I'm not making it up.

I ask her if she wants to go with me to Red Rock Canyon once I get a free day, and she doesn't say no. She has never been. I tell her driving there is like driving anywhere away from Oklahoma City, like you are floating on top of a pale rumpled green and yellow ocean. But then you turn off the highway and off the road and you are following a new path that corkscrews gently down, into the earth, like riding falling water, and there are trees and cool bright red-orange walls of stone rising over you from every direction, and it feels strange, and even a little frightening, and also peaceful, like in a good dream when you realize you're dreaming. But you aren't dreaming. The world exists.

GOOGLE informed me that one of the prerequisites I need for pre-nursing, a General Biology, is running in Summer I, in the mornings at OCCC, and there is space.

It is very difficult.

Taking the class is not a poem. It is a classroom—blank and purple and beige—too early in the morning, four days a week. The air conditioning is turned up too high. There are no windows. My chair has wheels and there is nowhere to roll to. The textbook is shiny as a new car; it is full of tiny long words, and diagrams of things I have never seen that I will have to understand. The professor is a father whose children have left home. He is very organized and doesn't make jokes or any more eye contact than necessary.

I keep myself in the chair. I know ahead of me in the day after class is work: shopping carts in the parking lot, dry fingertips, numbers. Then: traffic, beautiful storms, music at a volume loud enough to make the traffic hear or the radio on to bad news I listen to as hard as I can. Then a house with death in it. A few hours or at least a few words with Jane. And then another day, and another day and another day. Each morning is an empty and open hand.

acknowledgments

I want to thank all the writers who have helped me over the years, as teachers and readers and both. In particular, Karen Skolfield, Corwin Ericson, Stephanie Vaughn, Maureen McCoy, Michael Koch, Barry Matthews, Mark Rader, Maggie Vandermeer, Patrick Somerville, Ben Warner, George McCormick, Steve Chang, Ian King, Matt DiGangi, Jon Roemer, Steve Yarbrough, Bobbie Ann Mason, Chris Harding Thornton, Michael Hawley, and Casie Dodd.

about the cover artist

Chad Reynolds is a poet and visual artist who recently moved with his family to the Boston area from Oklahoma City. His typewriter art has been featured in magazines and journals in the United States, Germany, and Denmark, has been used for the covers of two novels, and is held by private collectors on three different continents. He started making art on typewriters around 2015 as a way to kill time between customers while working with Short Order Poems, a performance-art poetry experience involving poets using typewriters to create poetry on demand for strangers.

In Oklahoma City, Reynolds was the cofounder of Penny Candy Books, an independent book publisher that highlighted diverse issues and life experiences in children's books. He has published five chapbooks of poetry.

about the art

"in the morning, the city is the prairie" uses four colors and four marks on a Fredrix primed canvas. The first mark (the mark down at the bottom) is a yellow period; the second mark is an orange colon; the third is a red apostrophe; and the fourth is a purple plus sign. The orange mark comes in about two-thirds of the way up the yellow, the red comes in about two-thirds of the way up the orange, and so on. The marks increase in number by four in each of their first thirty-four lines until, at line thirty-four, they occupy each of the 132 spaces in a row. From that point on, each mark/color assumes the full row up through the top of the piece. The marks are distributed equally across each line to achieve the effect of a gradation from the bottom to the top.

ROB ROENSCH is the author of the novella *The World and the Zoo* (Outpost19) and the story collection *The Wildflowers of Baltimore* (Salt). He lives in Oklahoma City and teaches at Oklahoma City University.

IN THE MORNING, THE CITY IS THE PRAIRIE
was designed, edited, and typeset by
Belle Point Press in Fort Smith, Arkansas.
The text is set in Verdigris MVP Pro.

The mission of Belle Point Press is to celebrate the
literary culture and community
of the American Mid-South:
all its paradoxes and contradictions,
all the ways it gets us home.
Visit us at
www.bellepointpress.com.

BELLE
POINT
PRESS

Fort Smith, Arkansas